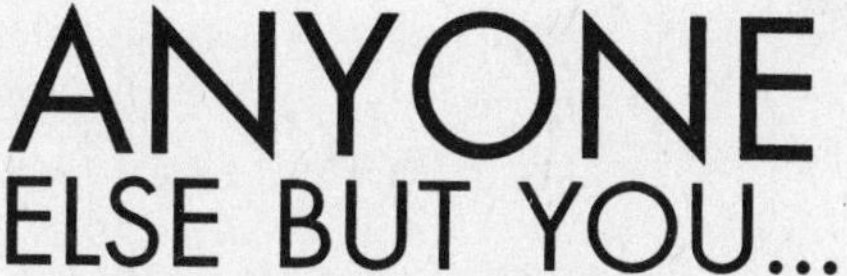

would understand that it's not life! It's a freakin' game!

ANYONE ELSE BUT YOU...

would understand that it's not life! It's a freakin' game!

Ritwik Mallik • Ananya Verma

Srishti
PUBLISHERS & DISTRIBUTORS

Srishti Publishers & Distributors
N-16, C. R. Park
New Delhi 110 019
srishtipublishers@gmail.com

First published by Srishti Publishers & Distributors in 2012

All characters in this book are fictitious, and any resemblance to real persons, living or dead, is coincidental.

Typeset in AGaramond 12pt. by Suresh Kumar Sharma at Srishti

Printed and bound in India

To Aditi,

And to those little flowers named Ashmi and Udita…

Life... is like a box of chocolates - a cheap, thoughtless, perfunctory gift that no one ever asks for, unreturnable because all you get back is another box of chocolates. So, you're stuck with mostly undefinable whipped mint crap, mindlessly wolfed down when there's nothing else to eat while you're watching the game. Sure, once in a while you get a peanut butter cup or an English toffee but it's gone too fast and the taste is fleeting. In the end, you are left with nothing but broken bits filled with hardened jelly and teeth-shattering nuts, which, if you are desperate enough to eat, leaves nothing but an empty box of useless brown paper.

~ The X-Files

Life is a game that must be played.

~ Edwin A. Robinson

Acknowledgments

Writing a book is never easy and more so when you have to juggle it between your studies and extra-curriculars. So, the entire support system that helps me bring this book to you should be the ones acknowledged really. In comparison to their contribution, I haven't done much really – just added a few words here and there and made the story readable.

My parents form the backbone of this support system and without their guidance and motivation; it'd be really hard for me to continue writing. A big hug to my elderly grandparents – both my grandmothers have played the role of efficient PR managers and *my grandfathers* have always egged me to follow my heart. The attempts made by my *maternal grandmother* to translate my works into Bengali and the publicity provided by my *paternal grandmother* for both my books, have been commendable.

Lots of love to my *Appa, Mamu-Mami & MumMum-Cream dadu*. I'm ever grateful to *my aunt* in Jersey, who has made sure that people read my books in the US too. All my *uncles and aunts* deserve a big mention for the way they've supported me all throughout and so do my army of *cousins*.

I extend my heartfelt gratitude towards all my teachers who've truly inspired me at every sphere of my life. And some of the mentions I'd want to make here: The ever amazing *Mrs. Gurleena Sikka*, who has always backed me during the worst of times; *Mrs. Rekha Jha*, for pointing out my shortcomings in the sweetest manner possible; *Ms. Renu Saxena*, for being like a mother at all times and for pampering me whenever I ran short on cash to treat my valentine; *Mr. Puneet Sharma*, for teaching me what it is like to be dedicated towards a purpose and the ever inspiring and supportive, *Mrs. Arpita Sen, Mr. Kannan, Mr. Beniwal, Mr. Ashish Singhal* and *Mr. Santosh Gupta.*

My existence would be in jeopardy if the likes *Himanil, Mayank* and *Srishti* weren't there for me. It is hard to imagine how hard it'd be to do anything without constantly asking them for advice.

Lots of love to a certain *Daksha,* for being there and making my life so much more beautiful. You are really really special, idiot. Remember that always...

A big thank you to *Aditi Verma, Runjhun Sharma, Siddhartha Sinha* and *Mihir Paul.* I extend my warm regards to the ever loving, *Ira ma'am* for agreeing to go through my manuscript and point out the flaws in it.

My publishers have made me what I am and I am indebted to them for the rest of my life. From the MD to the person who packages my books, every single person deserves credit for this work. *Sumit Sharma* needs a mention for the wonderful covers he makes. And not to forget my benevolent readers who keep on showering their best wishes and support at all times, I love each one of you.

And lastly, I'd like to thank my co-author *Ananya* – for trying to teach me the art of perfection. Her constant jibes on my faulty grammar and "melodramatic" writing style have made me improve leaps and bounds. With all the workload, it'd be hard to imagine how I could singlehandedly go through with this book.

I sincerely hope that you all enjoy this story and accept it like the way you have accepted *'Love Happens Like That'* and *'Because You Loved Me..'* into your lives.

Ritwik Mallik

My sister, I kid you not, is the best. Thank you for just being there. I cannot begin to thank you for all the times you've saved my a**.

I'd want to thank my co-author *Ritwik Mallik*, who has given me the opportunity of writing this book with him. Although it is very hard to make him listen to what I am saying, he was pretty patient when it came to this book. Only we know what ups and downs this book has been through.

I would like to thank my parents for helping me out whenever I have sought help.

My existence would be incomplete had it not been for my best friend. Thank you for being there always, for putting up with me. We will always have that weird connection, like we do, always.

Heartfelt gratitude to my teachers who have been there for me and have always encouraged me.

This is my first step into the world of writing and I hope that all of you enjoy reading this as much as we enjoyed bringing this to you.

All the best!

Ananya Verma

*This story is purely a work of fiction. As a result, any resemblance to a person, living or dead is purely co-incidental. The names of characters, places and organizations are **all fictional** in nature and they have been used without any ill-will.*

Authors

Prologue

The aroma of freshly picked daffodils filled the air as the sunlight peeped into her office through the tinted window pane. Mrs. Meena Singhal paced the floor of her office in anticipation of some good news. She walked towards the window that overlooked the lush front lawns of the school and stood for a moment to admire its' beauty. When she had first entered this school as a Physics teacher, seventeen years back – it was this very lawn and its beauty that had caught her attention. The dream to be the Principal and the passion for the job of teaching was as strong then as it was now but something about the school, its' lawns, the then-Principal's office had appealed to her and that appeal was yet to recede.

She had some fond memories of her first year, way back in the Summer of 1993. The then Principal, Mr. Chavan showed her around the school that was not yet fully built. Void of a Senior wing, she remembers how Mr. Chavan insisted that she put forward her ideas, her inputs and opinions regarding what all could be done to help the school expand and grow. The graciousness and display of respect by a Civilian Award recipient educationist towards an ordinary first-day teacher was commendable according to Mrs. Singhal. And she pledged that from that day on, she would not only be an excellent teacher but a warm hearted mother and an approachable friend to all the hundreds of students she would teach in years to come. And the results were instant, her popularity grew. Students swore by her name and in the process, the respect she was entitled to, became unmatchable. A couple of years later, she was entrusted with certain administrative responsibilities of that of a Coordinator which she fulfilled to perfection. A Head of the Department post followed and by the time she was about to complete her sixth year, she was already being talked about as a possible replacement for the soon to be retiring Mr. Chavan.

And the much expected call came; May 2000, Mrs. Meena Singhal officially took over as the Principal of the Delhi High School, thus taking over from a person, a premier educationist who had left behind a legacy of sorts. If one felt that the hard work had borne fruits, it wasn't to be as the hard work would now be needed.

A popular English news daily named the Truth of India started an annual award for the Best School and as expected Delhi High School won it a record 6 times in 7 years to become the first school ever to make it to the Hall of Fame.

And then the ominous signs, as Mrs. Singhal aged, the magic touch in her administrative abilities soon started diminishing. The popular and motivational leader soon began getting confused over her own theories. The man management capabilities were deteriorating and there was unrest everywhere. The calls for change grew louder as teachers and students alike wanted a relatively younger Principal to take over the reins. She believed that it was the best time for her to leave and so did many others including the Chairman of the trust, Mr. A.Chandrashekhar. She applied for a voluntary retirement from her active responsibilities of teaching and being the Principal of an institution. And in return she was offered the post of the Director of Delhi High Schools, which she gladly accepted.

A knock on the glass door of her cabin diverted all her attention from her past to her present.

"Come in," she said in a gentle voice.

Her teary eyed secretary walked in, "they've accepted it ma'am. So it's final then?"

Singhal pursed her lips, “Yes. And you should be happy that I am going before people ask me to go. The question is that they will say ‘why now?’ rather ‘why not?’.” Singhal could afford a smile. A lot of stress dropped from her shoulder, she could leave happily now and with her head held high.

She gracefully walked across her room towards her grand revolving chair. She sat down and took a sip of water. “So Sunaina…” she said.

“…I hope you will forgive me if I’ve ever given you a tough time over these 10 years that you’ve worked as my Secretary. I sincerely apologize.”

Ms. Sunaina wiped a bead of tear, “Not at all. It’s been an honour serving you.” Sunaina tried hard to put up a smile but failed miserably.

Almost immediately Singhal’s phone buzzed. It was the Chairman.

“Could you excuse me for a minute?”

Sunaina nodded and left.

Very few would know that the winds of change had begun to blow over Delhi High School.

ONE

A lot of commotion surrounded the Reception area of DHS. On a normal day you would find it to be deserted but the first round of interviews for Class XI had begun and hundreds of applicants had to be interviewed. Admission during this time of the year of the students of Class XI was of topmost priority for the school. It was so because those very students would be the face of the school, representing the prestigious institution for two years to come in every competition in different schools in different cities. Their results would be printed in the brochure of the school. They couldn't afford to take this lightly.

For the new-admissions, it was a chance to rub shoulders with the future IITians, businessmen and leaders of the country. It was a chance for them to bask in the glory of being a *Delhite* - a tag which is privileged to a few yet wanted by all. It was a chance to make new friends, enemies. A chance for girls to swoon over hot guys and as for teachers, it meant a fresh bunch of students with fresh ideas, handpicked to suit their standards of 'quality students'.

For Meena Singhal, it was her last responsibility as the Principal of a school she had dedicated a major part of her life working for. As for Rishav Sen it was a chance to fulfill a childhood dream of wearing the coveted bottle green blazer.

Tall, slim built, a little bit of stubble on his face, with a white shirt casually worn over a worn out jeans; Rishav Sen walked towards the door leading to the reception with careful steps. There was a hint of nervousness in his walk which he disguised with a confidence that only some would be able to see as what it was- superficial. He had achieved more than what a 16 year old would ever dream of – youngest writer to get published, former Junior Editor at the Truth of India.

He wasn't entirely new to the school, its lawns, its grand reception and the sense of being lost in the winding corridors seemed all too familiar. He could remember exactly where he had sat, six years ago in the same reception area. The chairs were green then. He was new to the city then. All he had was a not-so-impressive report card with average marks. On top of that he was applying mid-session.

For Rishav it was going to be sweet revenge. To walk around among those who had spurned him six years ago. It would totally be an "in-their-face" thing. He wanted to prove a point and he wasn't going to rest until he had done so. The pile of certificates in his hand should be enough he said to reassure himself.

Jai Chauhan fell on top of his bean bag with a thud. An hour of intense work out had drained every ounce of energy that he had. He barely managed to reach for his iPhone which was luckily lying somewhere close to his couch. He dialed the number of his personal caretaker and waited for him to answer.

He picked up after the first three rings.

"Omar *chacha*, *ek* Breezer *aur ek* packet chips *le aana*," he ordered in an exhausted voice and hung up even before Omar could reply in an affirmative. Jai knew that an order was an order and it was now up to Omar to arrange for what he asked. He turned on the Air conditioner with disdain as though His Royalty was doing a favour by allowing the Hitachi people to manufacture Air conditioners that would cool his sweaty body.

Jai lifted his t-shirt and observed his chiseled stomach. His abs were considerably well shaped now and he decided to name them after six random Wonders of the World. His next prey was the television set which he glanced spitefully at. *You tiny screened bastard*, he thought. It had been seventeen attempts since he had successfully managed to scale a level in the popular war game, Call of Duty and he took it upon his moral obligation to blame his 32" television (which he considered small by his standards) for every wrong button pressed as a result of his born incompetence.

The television was on, Xbox plugged in, Air-conditioner producing a chilling effect and his favourite falvour of potato wafers and Breezer beside him, the stage was set for Jai to exhibit his *jainess* and so he did. He clumsily ate the chips, took gulps of the Breezer in between and left his Commando to fend for himself in the game. And every time he lifted the analog to move further, his hungry stomach called for his attention. And as a result of which, his poor commando (who had already experienced 23 rebirths before that) continued to be denied *moksha,* over and over and over again.

Jai Chauhan surprisingly was one of the model students of Delhi High School. He was the incumbent to the post of the Head Boy. A shocking transformation in the ape that he was to a more civilized form of a human being led to his teachers living under the illusion of Jai being a direct descendent of the old man who lived in Vatican City and ruled the hearts of a million with his holiness.

Singhal keenly observed the young boy's face, the one who was sitting in front of her. She could see that he was trying to be confident. *He tries too hard,* she thought. *If only he would just loosen up a little bit, it'll do wonders. His application is quite impressive though.* For an ordinary person, the boy would seem over- confident and too much into himself. But years of experience had made reading the micro-expressions of a student, cakewalk for her. She could sense a little bit of arrogance in his voice. But he was polite.

It'd be interesting to have him in this school. Too bad I won't be there to see what becomes of him, she thought

Rishav on the other hand sat with goose-bumps on his arms. It wasn't even that cold in there. *Weird,* he thought. But he quickly regained his composure, ready to answer what was asked of him.

He was totally in awe of the lady in front him. *She looks so calm. Not judgmental about students,* he noticed. He couldn't read anything from her face. It was contemplative. A little pucker between her eyes appeared as she scanned the application intensely. Like there was nothing more important than that. He thought it to be a privilege to be studying in a school that was being run by a person of Mrs. Meena Singhal's stature and caliber.

The classroom sized Principal's cabin seemed smaller than what it appeared the day Singhal received the news that her retirement request was accepted. It was far more cramped than usual. Mainly due to the presence of eight different teachers who were an integral part of the Selection Committee.

On the extreme left sat Ms. Veenu Sharma (Vice Principal 1), next to her was Dr. Madhuri Singh (Vice Principal 2). On either side of Mrs. Singhal were Mrs. Neeti Chopra (Headmistress) and Ashish Dutta (Mathematics). Apart from them, there was the unimportant bunch consisting of a megalomaniac Physics teacher, a demented English teacher and a stern looking Economics person.

"Please go ahead," Singhal directed the Eco teacher to start.

Rishav expected some subjective questions but to his utter surprise, the first question was totally something he was not prepared for. "Rishav, can you please differentiate between growth and development?" Now, that's what you call a bolt out of the blue! He wanted to ask whether they had seen the certificates. *Aren't they going to ask about my achievements?*

His throat was dry and it seemed his façade of confidence had shattered into a million or maybe a zillion pieces. "Ma'am, uhh.. I beg your pardon?" he tried to buy time.

"What's the difference between growth and development?" The stern looking lady repeated, with a hint of annoyance.

So much for patience, he thought.

"Growth…ummm…uhhh….uh….well.. It can be of two types!" Rishav thought on his feet.

"…physical and mental. It can relate to growth of human body or growth of a plant." *Wait, that makes it one. Wow, Rishav! So much for getting sweet revenge. Make a fool of yourself and get yourself kicked out of the school gates again.*

The Economics teacher smiled. One could hardly tell if it was genuine or sarcastic.

Nonetheless since she didn't stop him, he continued to say crap.

"You see ma'am," he began. "Growth, it is unidirectional. But development is a sense of all round development, a relative positive or negative change in the initial position of a person. It can be betterment or...."

"Tch tch," Rishav thought he heard the Eco teacher make that noise. She shook her head.

"Nevermind Rishav," the Headmistress smiled. The smile was genuine. "Tell me, when do we say that a pair of linear equations does not have any solution?"

Cakewalk, babe, he thought. Math was one of his strong points. "When a1/a2 is equal to b1/b2 but is not equal to c1/c2. A1, b1, a2, b2 being the coefficients of the variables and c1, c2 being the constants in the given two equations"

Rishav waited to see her response in baited breath. Even in the board exam he hadn't written in so much detail. Not even missing a single point. She nodded in approval. Relief washed over him.

He waited for a few moments to see if any more questions were going to be thrown towards him.

"Thank you, you may go," said Meena Singhal looking at the boy.

Rishav Sen got up and wished the teachers a good day, just like an obedient well bred and trained puppy. He stepped out of the Principal's cabin breathing a sigh of relief that it was finally over. *Whatever the result, at least I gave my best shot,*

That afternoon, when the list came out, the 26th name from the top was that of Rishav Sen. Despite the stammering and absolute bullshit he spoke inside, his not-so-successful interview didn't override his achievements. After all, they couldn't afford to not take in the youngest writer, could they?

TWO

The famed front loans sprang into action and this time it was to host the grand Farewell Dinner Party of the long serving Principal of DHS, Mrs.Singhal.

The party which was organized to bid Singhal goodbye came to be known for a number of firsts. For starters, the Chairman, A. Chandrashekhar gave a short speech, the loud Principal of Delhi High School International was low key, the mikes didn't malfunction, there was enough food for the hunger stricken guests, the lawn seemed neat and tidy, no-one had a runny nose in the choir and the greatest of them all was the never before seen camaraderie between the Heads of DHS who sat in a close huddle probably gossiping or discussing the brand of cosmetics they use. What surely appeared to a person observing them from a distance seemed to be a moderated discussion on the threat Pakistan's Nukes possessed in wake of the unstable Government that ran Pakistan.

"Meena, did you get to know about who's replacing you?"

Neeti asked with a lot of curiousness hoping against hope that she be promoted second time in 2 months and this time to become the Principal.

Madhuri popped in a question, “Is it anyone from our school?”

Veenu who was totally clueless about the topic of discussion and submerged in her own thoughts, decided to ask something as irrelevant as - “does my hair look bouncy today?”

None bothered to pay attention to the question of hers and instead decided to pay rapt attention to every syllable that came out of Singhal’s mouth. One could very well imagine how fruitful it would have been had all Heads (included: VP1, VP2 and HM) decided to pay half as much attention to Singhal while she was still running the show, it would have saved the typist the trouble of typing the retirement application and in turn would have allowed Singhal to fill her coffers for a few more years till she would retire gracefully in the truest terms.

Life was unfair, thought Singhal. And although she very well knew who’d be replacing her as the Principal; the bitch inside her prevented her from disclosing the name. Her much loved colleagues needed some thrill in life and that name would surely turn out to be a rude shock. And hence, Singhal got all the more reason to sit on the name.

“Might also be you, you know,” she looked at Dr.Madhuri.

“Or you maybe?” the very next instant her face was at Veenu, who clearly seemed disinterested in the post.

Singhal awakened the Socrates in her and started mumbling stuff like how anyone out of them would do justice to the job, how it really didn’t matter who was the Principal and how the school was like a family, etc. After all these years of displaying sanity, it seemed that it had deserted Singhal on the last night of hers at school.

Although most characters were around that evening when the champagne bottle was uncorked, one lady of eminence was indeed missing and she was Ms. Muskaan Kaur. In her mid forties, Muskaan Kaur was the princess-in-waiting to the throne of the Principal of Delhi High School. Conniving, shrewd and deadly; she possessed all qualities that would take her to the top. And those qualities weren't just for show but for functioning as well. An ordinary teacher, six years old in school got to use the Principal's standby car as a mode of transport – was anything else required to explicate the effect Muskaan had had on the crème de la crème of the Delhi High School Managing Trust? None questioned Muskaan's authority. Those who dared, never were seen again to tell the tale. An itchy wart, she had everything in her to make the toughest of people grimace in pain. She never wanted positions of authority as she had enough influence already. What she did want was an unfelt presence in every person's head. And she got that without effort, almost *everytime*.

"Where's Muskaan? I don't see her around." the Vice-Chairman pointed out loud, picking up his fifth glass of champagne.

A senior management member's interest in knowing the whereabouts of an ordinary (on paper) teacher sparked off a row of whispered conversations. And soon 'Who's the next Principal?' was replaced with a simpler question 'Where is Muskaan?'

Amidst the chaos that surrounded her absence, Muskaan Kaur unperturbed stood near the Ladies' Washroom of the reception, waiting for her colleague to finish with her flushing. The door knob turned and out came a lady in her early fifties, short, fat and with toad like features. She had dark rings of *kajal* below her eyes which made her look pretty much like an over-fed raccoon.

"It's dirty inside," the lady said laying undue stress on the alphabet 'S'.

"Is it?" Muskaan asked in a hoarse tone.

The lady nodded and walked ahead with Muskaan tottering behind.

"So what do you suggest Bindu? Should we make the announcement today?" Muskaan asked.

"No..." the lady called Bindu had a techno voice. It reminded one of the way Martians spoke in movies.

"...we need to wait," she finished.

"Why not today? Everyone would be drunk by the end of the party. It would be ideal I tell you, do you have issues with Chandra? If yes, then I can speak to him." Muskaan left no stone unturned in reminding Bindu about her proximity to the Chairman.

"It is not about Chairman Sir, it is not even about Meena, I don't think this occasion warrants an announcement. What's the harm in waiting?" Bindu inquired.

"Can't you understand what kind of a demoralizing affect it can have on the likes of Veenu and Madhuri? See sense BK. I know you've been out of touch all these years, but you got to trust me on this," she added a few words in a Punjabi dialect.

Bindu stopped surging ahead with the speed of an ostrich like she was a moment back. Now, she stood her ground, shifted her gaze towards Muskaan's cold eyes.

"Are you sure?" Bindu asked, yet again laying unnecessary stress on the alphabet 'S'.

Muskaan placed her hand on Bindu Kalsi's arm, "Trust me. I

won't let you down."

A few hundred meters away, the conspicuous absence of Muskaan had become a hot topic of discussion. Mr. A. Chandrashekhar trotted towards the table where all the Heads of DHS were seated. On seeing him, Neeti Chopra instantly got up to offer her chair which he politely refused.

"Can I have a word with you Meena?" He asked. "...alone," which was an immediate addition to his sentence.

Meena Singhal got up and both of them moved a few paces towards the counter where the bottles of mineral water were arranged.

"Meena, you have to make the announcement to your Staff before you leave. I don't want rebellions here." He coughed.

"As far as my knowledge was concerned, a couple of months back Sir, you were the very person who suggested that my continued presence would cause an internal revolt. What's with the new Principal being a cause of that?" Singhal minced no words.

"It's not that Meena. You are yet to realize why I am circumspect about our new Principal. You know *na* she's been out for long and with experienced and senior hands like Madhuri around, it might get difficult for her to work if the Staff doesn't take it down too well."

"You mean to say, that you didn't take any feelers from the staff before deciding upon who succeeds me?" Singhal was shocked.

"Of course I did. But two random staff members aren't the representative of the entire teaching faculty. And besides, I had thought about your idea of promoting Madhuri but try to understand, as the Chairman of the Trust – I am in many ways answerable to its' founder member, who in this case is the father of the person who is succeeding you." He avoided Singhal's gaze.

"You were pressurized?"

"Of course I wasn't. An entire Board took the decision for Christ's sake," Chandrashekhar for the first time lost his cool.

"You knew and so did the Board that Madhuri was the best person for the job, why this lady all of a sudden?"

A.Chandrashekhar chose not to reply. After a few seconds of silence he spoke, "Will you or will you not make the announcement to your staff Meena? Delay your departure by a day and hold a Staff Meeting to make the announcement, don't leave it to others to make the announcement."

And just then, there was a loud screeching noise and the loudspeakers roared to life, "May I have your attention please," it was the impeccable English accent of Ms. Muskaan Kaur.

The buzz in the audience died down as all eyes turned towards the elevated platform that was set up to act as a stage.

"As a member of the teaching faculty of Delhi High School, it'd be an honour for me to call up on stage, Mr. A.Chandrashekhar, our respected Chairman Sir to duly announce the name of the person who is all set to carry the flame of DHS forward and hence take forward the legacy of Mrs.Singhal. Sir if you may?" Muskaan moved away from the podium towards the left of the stage gesturing the Chairman to join her.

The announcement came as a bolt out of the blue for the Chairman. Just a moment ago, he was persuading Mrs. Singhal to delay her departure so that the name of the new Principal could be announced just at the right moment and the very next moment, he finds himself adjusting the height of the mike and clearing his throat – in readiness to announce the very same name.

Considering how embarrassing it might look, in utter dismay, the Chairman slowly made his way onto the stage.

"Thank you Muskaan for giving me this privilege to announce the name of the next Principal of DHS," a plastic smile followed.

There was silence all around as the Chairman took his time to frame his sentence.

"Twenty eight years ago, her father started off this Trust from his small apartment in East Delhi. And soon it grew into a reputed name in the field of providing quality education to one and all. It was her father, the erstwhile Principal of this school and the founder member of the DHS Trust who initiated this great legacy. And who better than his own daughter to carry it forward? I take this moment in time to announce that the new Principal of Delhi High School is none other than the daughter of Mr. Chavan, Mrs. Bindu Kalsi," The last few lines were well spaced out to take in audience response conveniently.

A large round of applause engulfed the front lawns of Delhi High School. And as the clapping died down, there was sense of insecurity amongst all present. The times were changing and so were the camps, one didn't know who to rally around and who to trust. No-one spoke a word apart from the customary 'It-was-shocking' looks. Dr. Madhuri Singh had already began cracking a few complex algorithms in her head, if someone felt deeply cheated then it was her.

THREE

Rishav scanned the huge space called the Multipurpose Hall to look for a suitable place to sit. He neither wanted to appear desperate nor a creepy loner. He chose a strategic seat in the middle. Not too close to the teachers, not too close to the backbenchers. The hall was partially filled but the flurry of students didn't stop. Three-fourth of the entire Class XI was already there while the rest were strolling their way across. There was the usual chatter that filled the air. The old friends were catching up. There was a lot to say, a lot to hear. It had been only a month after the Board exams but seemed like an eternity to the people who had gone away, some who had stayed, some who had just relaxed after one whole year of slogging.

Looking at those people laugh, Rishav felt nostalgic but tried hard to not remind himself of his friends in his alma mater. It was the first day of Class XI and like any other new kid, it was his first day and all he wanted to do was observe. Observe the body language of the students, to hear the slang that was used out here, to see the way they behaved with the teachers. He wanted to fit in as soon as possible. He didn't want to stand out for the wrong reasons.

Loud thuds on the wooden flooring of the hall echoed in backdrop of immediate silence. The new principal of DHS had arrived, Bindu Kalsi closely followed by Madhuri, Veenu and Neeti walked into the Hall in a haste. The students, a minute ago unaware of the uncommanding presence, stood up to greet the new *princi.*

"Please be seated," Kalsi took the microphone as everyone sat down with a noise of the moving chairs.

"Good morning..." she began with what was supposed to be her 'short' introductory speech.

It was the first time she was addressing the students of *her* school. She planned to make it an impressive one.

Yeah not as impressive as Meena Singhal, thought Rishav. *She had a weird charm of sorts. She had an aura. A good one. Of respect and awe.* And that is what exactly the students were thinking. They noticed every minute detail of her attire, her hair, her sandals, her height, the indents on her cheeks, the deep- badly- applied- kajal. They couldn't help but laugh at the way she was stammering. The students of DHS weren't shy to comment on any of the peculiar things about a person. The person who first saw it and pointed it out was the one who got everyone's attention. And much to the picked-on-person's chagrin, the person who pointed it out was the one who also got everyone's approval.

When her speech finished, the people clapped more out of gratitude for finishing with the speech rather than applauding her for her incoherent tone and over-repeated statements.

"She is not that bad," the guy sitting next to Rishav said.

"Yeah. Not that bad," he replied.

"I am Siddhant by the way."

"Rishav," he said, extending his hand.

"I have been here for two years only. I hope the new Principal does something and doesn't just sit around," Siddhant said.

"Why? The previous one? Didn't she do anything?" Rishav asked.

"Well, she was pretty relaxed. Not much was going around."

"Oh. I thought otherwise."

"Anyway, let's see what this one is like."

"Okay then. Which stream?"

"Commerce with Maths. And you?" Siddhant asked.

"Humanities it is."

"Move out of the MP Hall in a single file," a teacher shouted on the microphone

"Let's go then." Rishav said.

"Okay. It's break time. You wanna see around?"

"Yeah sure, why not? I'd love to!" Rishav replied with enthusiasm.

Rishav was pleased that he had made atleast one friend on his first day. It's never too good to be alone.

And he was doubly happy that that friend was genuinely nice.

FOUR

Sahana was late. *When was she not?* She asked herself. But just because you are one freakin minute late doesn't mean you close the doors on the face of a person. She stared at the guard, making a face. She had zero tolerance for people who did not understand logic. And she couldn't bother to explain people things because; well it was too much of an effort. And plus she had no patience. Not even a teensy little bit.

She yawned with her mouth totally open, just as a black car stopped by her.

She looked at it with surprise, but was ready to fight with all her might in case someone was trying to kidnap her. *Haha,* she thought. *Kidnapping me? I am not even a penny's worth.*

She chucked the idea and waited for the tinted window to slide down. A woman with a squished face and mouth in a pout looked up.

"You are late on the first week of school," she said.

Sahana raised her eyebrows and just stared at the woman.

She couldn't think of anything to say to a woman whom she didn't know and who pointed to her that she was late.

After a minute she just managed to shrug.

"Let her in," she said to the guard.

Okay, then. Must be a new teacher, I guess.

A few minutes later she dumped her bag on a desk. She took out a hair brush and kept it into a pocket and rushed to the washroom.

She saw all the girls chitchatting and immediately spotted her friend, Vanya.

"I don't know why strange things happen to me" she said as she opened her hair to comb.

"Hieee!! How are you?" Vanya jumped.

"I am good. What about you?" Sahana replied.

"Nothing much. Just that I went to Indonesia and saw the cutest guy possible."

"Whoa, woman! Why do you always see hot guys and I whereas don't even come near on, EVER?" Sahana exclaimed.

"Well, that's called bonne chance. And what strange thing, by the way?"

"This stupid ugly woman in this strange black car stopped next to me. I got scared *ki pata nahin kaun hai.* I was ready to put up a fight when the window slid open and this ugly lady with *kajal* smeared over face said "You're late for school on the first day" I *toh* couldn't say anything. I just shrugged and she ordered the guard to open the door and he did. I was so relieved that she was a teacher. Phew!" Sahana explained.

"Hahaa. Good that it was a teacher. But it would've been more fun if it were this weird little witch who had come to warn you not to come late to school. It's God's way to tell you to wake up early, Sahana. I think you should listen to Him," Vanya teased.

"Oh shut up," she said as they walked out of the bathroom.

FIVE

The loud bell of DHS rang, spreading cheer all round. Teachers raised their eyebrows at their apparent joy but nobody could give a damn about them. But the end of the Political Science period in class XI G made Rishav curse the noise. He was almost done with buttering the new subject, back and forth when the noisy- cheery bell rang.

Damn. Rishav thought. He had bragged a little. Well, a lot. But in these times you can't get noticed without tooting your horn can you? He waited for the right opportunity to start up a conversation. And when he got his chance he couldn't stop. Going from one thing to another; Offering his opinion and listening to hers too. *Although I couldn't give a rat's ass about what you thought about Salman Rushdie*, he thought. But he had to care. He praised her and then thanked her for complimenting him in a not-so-modest way. And just when he was going to ask about her family and tell her about his lineage, the bell rang.

"I would love to stay and chat but I've got some work to do. I'll talk to you later, Rishav," the lady named Mrs. Sunita smiled and spoke.

"Okay, ma'am. See you later."

Sweeeet victory, he smiled in his thoughts.

"Too hard. Trying, I mean... too hard," the girl who sat closest to the door spoke.

Rishav turned; intrigued that someone was closely observing him. "Really?" he asked, raising an eyebrow

The girl smiled with a tilt of her mouth.

"101 Ways to Impress a Teacher' - someone gifted it to me. Borrow it from me sometime. Handy tips," Rishav smirked.

The girl got up, "Sure babe. I will borrow it the day I want to be like you; which let me warn you now, won't ever come. New?"

"Yeah. You were here in tenth?" he asked

"Yeah," Sahana said curtly while she got up from her seat and turned to go towards the door.

"Rishav. And you are?" a short pause followed.

"Sahana. You know, you need to pick out the targets for your buttering with utmost care. There are around hundred here. And you can't impress all of them. Unless you address them in the M.P. Hall and tell them all about yourself."

"Haha. You know, I actually won't mind that. It's pretty convenient, you see," Rishav followed Sahana as she ambled her way out of the class towards the corridor.

"I am telling you. You are wasting your time on non-consequential people."

"Really?" they had reached the staircase which led to the top floor.

"*Really*," Sahana said with sarcasm. "But for god's sake at least make it less apparent. Teachers aren't *that* dumb," She walked ahead of him. "Or maybe they are," she said, giving him a meaningful look.

"It all works out to my advantage. And there's no harm in a little bit of buttering. And everyone likes to be praised. Even if it's not true. Human nature it is. Where are you going anyway?" Rishav asked her as he followed her into the maze of corridors.

"Where I want to."

"And the place being?" he followed it up.

"….my friend's classroom. She's in Commerce."

Sahana walked with haste.

"What's the hurry?" Rishav asked, biding for time.

"Break is for freaking 20 minutes. Five minutes the teacher takes. Five minutes early the next teacher arrives. Leaves us with exactly ten minutes to eat and meet people. Bloody, stupid school system."

"Ohkay. So that's why you are rushing. No-one ever bothered to tell the teachers about this thing?"

"The only time the teachers will talk about anything, apart from studies, is break; which we can't afford to waste."

"…and then you complain," he chipped in.

"Excuse me?" Sahana abruptly turned around and raised a finger. "It's your first week. You know crap about this school. You have no right to judge. When you have spent 10 years in this school, then maybe you are allowed to say that. As for what I just said, I was purely kidding. We've told them. But they are reluctant. What else can we do?"

"Okay, okay. My bad. Sorry?" Rishav said, with an apologetic face.

"You better be," Sahana said and walked off.

The break was over. The teacher hadn't come yet. Rishav sat near the windowsill with his book, trying to read it. But to his annoyance, he couldn't. He looked at the page full of words and kept looking at the words instead of reading the sentences.

All he could think about was the stupid conversation with Sahana.

I've managed to create one enemy. Not that bad, Rishav, he thought.

He looked at the page again. He couldn't bother to hold that book in his hand anymore. He put his bookmark on that page and kept it on his desk. He was about to get up and go to the washroom, since he had nothing else to do, when Sahana entered with her friend.

He sat on his chair again. He thought of all the ways of approaching her but decided against it.

Not in front of her friend, he thought. *Wait for the friend to go. Then, maybe. Till then, read the book. Yes. That is much better.*

He opened his book again, blankly staring at the page. He tried to read the first sentence. *Makes sense,* he thought. He continued to read it, when he was interrupted by her voice. "Nice bookmark," she said.

"Thanks," Rishav replied with a smile, wondering why she, herself came to talk to him when clearly she was pissed a little while ago.

"So you forgave me."

"What?"Sahana asked, puzzled.

"I said sorry. You walked off. But you are talking to me right now. So you forgave me?"

"Well...you could say that. Everyone's allowed one mistake. You made yours. And you are new. I didn't want to give you a hard time. It's difficult, I know. I've been there."

Rishav raised his eyebrows wondering at how hotheaded she seemed a few minutes ago and how understanding she was now.

"Thanks. It is pretty hard. What's with the corridors, I don't get. Why don't they have signs? It's such a confusing place."

She laughed. "I've been there too. I have changed four schools. This is the fifth. I always used to forget the way to my classroom, so this time I had decided to remember it. I remembered the way... and the number of stairs too. On the second day I ended up climbing the same stairs four times. The first time I went, I saw the piece of paper above the door. 9B was written on it. I went down again - counted the number of stairs. And then, came up again to find myself exactly at the same place. I did this four times. Until this girl came and said *'Sahana, where are you going? Our class is here'*. That was 9B. But actually it hosted 7D," Sahana explained.

Rishav laughed.

"You were a stupid kid," he said.

"I was new, okay? All these people were so intimidating that I was afraid to ask them. What if they took me to a corner and ragged me, like I had heard?" Sahana said with a defiance.

"You were paranoid too," Rishav said.

"If you were there, you would've known," Sahana said with a little hint of anger.

Rishav tried to change the subject hurriedly; afraid he would make another mistake, which he couldn't afford to make.

"So you came here in seventh?"

"Yeah. Bad year. Don't ask," she replied looking out of the window.

"First year is always bad. It's when you are getting the hang of things."

"Yes," she said with a distant look in her eyes.

A silence prevailed.

"You better hope that your first year is not bad since you have only two years here," Sahana said with a playful hint.

"Well then I need someone who could help me get the hang of things around here," Rishav said, with a hope that Sahana would get the hint of what he was trying to imply.

"I can tell you what *not* to do. But *'what to do'* depends upon which of the cliques in our school you wanna belong to, you know?"

"What is that supposed to mean?" Rishav asked.

"See, we have a lot of groups in our school. There's the 'Geek and Nerd Group'. These people are the ones who are in science and computers both. We have the 'Council Group'. These are the ones who aspire to be in the Council of this school, over achievers, basically. Then we have the 'Gossip Group'. You know, what that group contains. We have the 'Freak Group'. This is where the non-academic and non-anything people are. And we have the 'Middle Group'. These interact with the gossip, a little bit of geek group, and with the council. So which one do you wanna be in?"

"Let me think. Which one do you belong to?" Rishav asked.

"None," Sahana replied with a shrug of her shoulders.

"Huh? How is that possible?" Rishav inquired.

"Why would it not be? See, according to me I don't fit in anywhere. I have friends. I don't care of whatever group they belong to. It's a stupid concept. Although, it's not like all these groups don't talk to each other. They do. But they just don't hang out with each other," Sahana explained.

"Wow. I didn't know that," Rishav said.

"Why? Weren't there any cliques in your school?" Sahana asked.

"There were, but not so much. Or maybe I didn't notice," Rishav replied, trying to remember what it was like in his previous school.

"I think this all started with watching those movies like *Mean Girls* or whatever. Some were so influenced by it that they also wanted something like that. And they did. But now, it's not that much, because all such people have gone."

"Good for us," Rishav smiled.

"Yep! Good for us," Sahana replied.

The teacher came and Sahana went back to her seat.

SIX

The tube lights of the conference room flickered to life. Next was the AC which started efficient cooling within moments of it being turned on. A beautifully decorated flower vase adorned the centre of the 50 seater conference table. The chairs smelt of polish and the room of vanilla. Just about then, the doors to the room creaked open and Madhuri and Kalsi walked in.

Kalsi seemed sluggish in her walk. Her eyes reflected a kind of soreness that could have only been visible due to lack of sleep. Madhuri on the other hand displayed anxiousness. She was nervy and tense. They took two seats closest to the door.

"When will the staff arrive?" Madhuri asked adjusting her spectacles.

Kalsi stared back at her as though a highly insulting question had been asked, "I presume we discussed it yesterday itself Madhuri."

"Oh yes, yes, I remember now." Madhuri recollected the timing in her head. "Do you have good news for me?" Madhuri knew that it was hardly plausible to ask Kalsi this question when the entire staff would be present. Hence, it seemed ideal to pop in the question now and let Kalsi have a feeler of things to come. Knowing Kalsi's habit of keeping things close to her chest, deep within Madhuri existed a feeling that she would not really get the answer she was looking for.

"You need to understand Madhuri..." Kalsi started off with her squeaky and incomprehensive tone. "There are a lot of things one needs to take into consideration while appointing someone the post of the Principal. It is not really entirely in my hands you see..." Kalsi paused to notice the change in expression on Madhuri's face. Kalsi had to be clever; she had to camouflage her autocratic tendencies with clear cut diplomacy. And it was as difficult as asking Hitler to let his daughter marry a Jew.

"But Bindu dear, I think you are the supreme authority there at Greater Delhi High School. Isn't the Director supposed to call the shots?" Madhuri tried to prod Kalsi's tremendous ego by reminding her of the powers she possessed as the Director of Greater Delhi High School which was located around twenty kilometers away. Madhuri thought that all Kalsi wanted was a reminder of her endless power and by boosting her ego, Madhuri would stand a chance of getting her work done.

"It is not an autocratic setup. Running a school isn't autocracy," Kalsi's left eye twitched while saying this. "I have weighed my options very carefully and in the end I have arrived at the right decision and I hope I'll be having your support on this Madhuri," she gazed at Madhuri expecting some kind of an affirmative reply. She waited for a silent assurance that Madhuri would accept any decision taken in the right spirit.

That assurance never came. Instead the door treated them to some loud knocking and an instant later, a head popped in, followed by the entire body. It was Veenu. "The staff is here," she announced.

Kalsi took in a deep breath of air, "Ask them in." She slightly adjusted her sari and then placing her hands on the table, propped up her heavy head with an evident look of reluctance.

Madhuri looked on apprehensively as the seats went on filling in one by one.

Heavy footsteps in the form of His Highness Jai Chauhan made its way across the 1st floor corridors of Delhi High School. A constant growling noise under his breath and a chimp's spine accompanied him as he walked past the innumerable students filling the corridors during the change of a period. The occasional - 'Sup bitch?' was followed by a hand shake or a back slap when he met a familiar face. In case it was a girl, the general mode of interaction would be to call out the name of a girl in different tones and voices. Otherwise, the royalty didn't really bother to look around for attention; he had got enough of it from the moment he was born. It was a matter of concern that so many, in fact most students looked upon Jai as a role model. And Jai in his *jainess* never cared a fuck about them. *Chutiya hai sab*, he would say and walk ahead in his arrogant strut.

Jai bumped into his good friend Hardik, on his way to class, "Fuck man! Where're you going?"

"Nowhere man, going to Madhuri's office. I got late today," Hardik made a puppy dog face.

Jai started laughing on hearing this, he even backslapped Hardik, "You will never change will you dog? Tell me once in four years, when you've come on time?"

Unkempt hair, spectacles hanging on his nose and unshaved,

Hardik searched for an answer but couldn't really come up with one convincing enough.

The year before, the school began at 7.30, Hardik woke up at 7.45. Soon, due to excessive heat during summers, the timings changed to 6.45 and Hardik woke up at 7.15. Then came winters, the school got delayed by an hour and a half to around 9. Even then, Hardik reached school a good twenty minutes late. In the last four years or so, it's been seldom that someone's *not* seen Hardik running into school late on time with disheveled hair and a constipated look on his face. Meena Singhal had got so tired of seeing Hardik's face every day that she soon shifted the responsibility of late comers to Veenu and Veenu after a month of dealing Hardik asked Madhuri to take over. By far this would be Hardik's sixth visit to Madhuri this month, if he managed to reach her office on time in the first place.

"Dude, you think Madhuri will scold me?" Hardik asked.

"Do you think that's even worth an ask? Of course she will, not unless she gets replaced," Jai replied.

"Replaced? Why man? Now why will she be replaced?"

Jai shook his head, "Look at this, this way. Every time you've been coming late continuously for a fortnight, at the end of it the person looking after the late-comers has either been shifted from duty or has voluntarily asked to be replaced. And I bet Madhuri has had enough of you." He chuckled.

"Not sure dude. *Tu chalega?*" Hardik asked unsure. "Man, you'll be the Head Boy; I'm sure she'll take your side and not take my case. *Chal na?*"

Jai contemplated the outcome of his actions. After deliberating, he realized that it would only help him earn his reputation of being a real students' representative in front of Madhuri and decided to tag along with Hardik.

As they made their way across towards Madhuri's office on the ground floor, they could see teachers coming out of the Conference room in flocks. "Some kind of meeting must be on," Jai said in a serious tone.

"Yes dude?"

"Yeah," Jai replied in affirmative. "Let's see if someone's there with Madhuri or not."

As they went closer to Madhuri's office they could hear her talking loudly on the phone. They went closer and peeped in through the small glass panel on her door. She was talking on the phone and nervously pacing her room.

She kept on repeating the word, "Unacceptable."

"What's wrong?" Hardik asked.

"Shhh...." Jai replied. He went a little closer towards the door so that he could get a better ear to what Madhuri was saying.

"It's over Sir..." came the voice. "...I have had enough of this place. It's time I go Sir. I am not required," Madhuri fell silent perhaps while hearing out the reply.

"You knew I was the best person for the job but you didn't intervene. You robbed me off this opportunity not once but twice," she seemed agitated. "I am done for good Sir. For good. That woman kept me on the tenterhooks for weeks together and this is what she says in the end? It's a big joke, that's what it is."

She went silent again, some more explanations were coming from the other end.

Madhuri heard him out and regained composure, "What's done is done Sir, you'll get my papers by today afternoon. I don't want to stay here a minute longer. Thank you for your support, duly acknowledged."

Jai was stunned to hear about the latest developments but he didn't dare to utter a word to Hardik who was standing just behind him, a little away. Madhuri ended the call and dialed another number, as it seemed from outside. "Forward me the resignation letter I typed last night," she said and hung up.

Jai turned around shell shocked. With Hardik's question-marked expression, Jai couldn't really keep this thing to himself. He walked along with Hardik slowly towards the ground. "Looks like your jinx isn't broken yet..." he said.

"Why?"

"Madhuri is being replaced. And not just from late-comers' responsibility; but for good," Jai finished his half sentence.

Hardik stared at him with an expression similar to his when he heard the news first. No-one knew what to do and how to react. But it was in their best interests that they kept the news to themselves.

SEVEN

Happy Birthday to you, Happy Birthday to you...Happy Birthday to Sahana, Happy Birthday to youuuu....!" There was a loud round of clapping and hooting after the chorus got over.

The knife ran through the delicate, creamy chocolate truffle cake and Sahana broke a piece of it and popped it into Vanya's mouth.

Vanya took a huge piece of cake and made Sahana eat half of it and rest of it went on her face. Sahana groaned as her best friends covered every inch of her face with chocolate cake. Others laughed as they watched both of them fight and laugh. They too fed her cake and of course rest of it went on her face.

Rishav stood there in one corner watching as a perfectly edible cake went on to spoil Sahana's pretty face. He didn't know whether to go and wish her among her old friends. He was awkward when it came to these things. He didn't know what to do in such situations. He had just talked to her for approximately half an hour, that too, a week ago. He wasn't sure whether this was enough to give her a card.

He had gone to a sector nearby, for running an errand for his mom when he remembered it was her birthday. He wondered what would be the appropriate gift for a person whom you had talked to for a little while. He ran his fingers through the categories of an array of cards in the Archies gallery. He looked for something that was not too expressive. *Just a simple birthday card.* He chose a simple card with cream background with a small blue bear on the right hand corner with a little bit of sparkle on it. It had no double meaning whatsoever. Just a cute little wood creature.

He took a black felt tip pen and wrote:

Last week, a candle factory burnt down and everyone sat around it to sing Happy Birthday. Well I really don't need to wait for something like that to happen to wish you a really HAPPY & AWESOME BIRTHDAY Sahana! Best wishes, Rishav.

The next day he was standing with the card in a yellow envelope clutched tightly his hand. He was wondering when her friends would leave her side and give her a moment alone so he could give her the card. He didn't want unnecessary eyebrow raising by her friends. That'd be just too much.

He waited for nearly an hour or so when Sahana was finally left alone by her friends. He quickly walked up to her and handed it to her. "Happy Birthday, I hope you like it," he said, looking down at the card and avoiding looking into her eyes.

"Wow, thank you. It's really nice of you to give a card to a person whom you've barely talked to." She smiled.

Rishav smiled, nodded and turned around and went to the bathroom since he had nowhere else to go.

After a few hours he found himself sitting near the windowsill, on the other side of the classroom, watching his new interest of sorts. He had had many interests in the pasts but this one was particularly intriguing. Sahana was talking to her friends, sitting on a desk with her back facing him. He sat there with a sadness. What kind he didn't know. There was this weird need to get up and go sit next to her. Obviously he wouldn't do that. But his mind was so restless, insistent upon doing so. He again opened his book to read. As he began to read, he forgot all about the classroom. All noise dimmed, people around him seemed to disappear as he was transported into the world of mystery, deceit and murder.

He was imagining the horror of rats cutting into the wounds of his legs when he was startled by the noise

"You want some cake?" Sahana asked him, with a box of chocolate cake in her hand.

"Sure," Rishav picked up a small piece, and smiled up at her.

"No. Take a bigger piece," Sahana said.

"How was your birthday?"

"You mean how *is* it? Because it still is April 29."

"Yeah yeah. So how many gifts? Party tonight?" Rishav asked inquisitively.

"No party. I don't live with my parents. And the people whom I live with aren't you know..." Sahana said without completing the sentence.

"They are conservative?" Rishav asked; glad to know some private detail of this complex matter sitting in front of him.

"To say the least. Anyway, I don't want to talk about it. Party in school is good enough for now. *Chalo*, I will talk to you later. I've gotta go. Bye," she said, getting up and waving her hand.

"Bye," he said - which was too late since she was already too far to hear that.

Hardik and Jai huddled up near the corner of the basketball court. From the onset of it, it appeared to be an intense discussion of what strategies they were going to implement while play was on. If one managed to get closer, apart from the smells of sweat and stale breath, what one would get to sense is the amount of restlessness that had taken over His Highness Jai regarding the incumbency of his Head Boy's post.

"Dude, why are you worried?" Hardik asked.

"Man, Madhuri Singh was a pet of mine..." Realising his mistake although it came from the interiors of his heart, he corrected it, "I meant I was a pet of Madhuri. The reason I could go about doing anything was because Madhuri was there. Now if she goes, there's a *big* question mark over my application dude."

Hardik nodded. "She was a support you know, a huge one. She could single handedly get me this post but now with Bindu around; I doubt what'll happen to me."

"New Vice Principal, you think?" Hardik asked.

"Not really. Considering how autocratic this lady is, she'll keep the group as core as possible. Maybe a promotion here and there but I doubt it whether we'll get a new VP" Jai's concern was evident in his mellowed down tone.

"Dude *tera toh katta ho gya*!" Hardik started laughing loudly.

"Motherfu*cker, shut up!!" Jai barked. "We need solutions here, not problems. You think I could get someone to side by me?"

"Veenu?" Hardik suggested.

"Veenu!" Jai exclaimed.

They knocked on the door. Veenu replied, "Come in."

Jai and Hardik walked into her cabin with their hands at their back.

"Morning ma'am," Jai said. Hardik mumbled.

Veenu nodded with a smile.

"What brings you here Jai? Missing me? Hehehheheheee…." The laughter seemed more of an afterthought.

"Ma'am actually I was inquiring about the Council and…" Jai started speaking.

"Wait, wait, do you know this boy?" Veenu interrupted the royalty even before he could complete his sentence. There would have been a million Hiroshimas happening within Jai at that moment.

Veenu pointed towards a boy whose presence wasn't noticeable as such, at least not to Jai and Hardik – the moment they entered.

"This is Rishav Sen, he's a new student. Your batch mate," Veenu introduced.

On being mentioned, Rishav faced Jai and Hardik and smiled.

"Oh, okay ma'am. Ma'am as I was saying that the Council needs to be…" Jai started off again.

"Listen *na*!" Veenu interrupted him again. This time there was going to be Pearl Harbour within Jai.

"Yes ma'am?" A clearly frustrated Jai asked.

"This boy Rishav, sweet boy he is. You should make friendship with him. He suggested that the top floor corridor is a hazardous prospect for the children because it is not covered. And there is no parapet, why didn't you guys notice that before?" She shot a question.

"Ma'am, erm erm…actually we were going to talk…" this was Jai's third try.

"Oh, wait. Rishav, this is Jai Chauhan, a very bright, intelligent and responsible student. One of the best we have in this school," She said proudly. "And I hope that you too join them in the list of responsible and bright students of this school."

"Will surely ma'am," Rishav nodded with gratitude.

A visibly flattered Jai couldn't really stop thinking about the words 'bright' and 'intelligent'. It was like two ads were running in his head simultaneously. One was of Surya lights and the other, Intel Processors.

"Yes, Jai…you were saying?" Veenu finally remembered that Jai was to complete what he had begun saying.

The royalty couldn't afford being snubbed a fourth time so he chose the easy way out, "Nothing really ma'am. Just came to say *hi*."

"Aaaw, how *sweet*," Veenu said as she opened her drawer. "Take this," she handed over to Jai a bar of Kitkat. Share it with your friend Hardik. She beamed with abnormal happiness.

"Right ma'am, I shall see you then." With his mission being nothing but a waste of time, Jai stepped out of Veenu's cabin with unparalleled gloom.

"Bloody *bangali*…!" he scowled. "Yo dude!" Hardik backslapped him knowing that a new kid taking away the spotlight from Jai wouldn't really have gone down too well with him.

No Madhuri and Veenu has a new poster boy…

Could life get any worse for Jai Chauhan?

EIGHT

The bartender was ready to show his skills in the luxury apartment of Jai Chauhan. Jai was hosting the pre Council party to garner student support for his council application. Everyone had assumed that Jai would host it. As for Jai, he didn't mind. After all he had to become the Head Boy. It was worth it.

Plus, he had another reason - to meet his ex- flame- Arzoo. He had still not gotten over her since she unceremoniously dumped him. Three months ago. He hoped that this would be the time when he won her back.

The terrace of Jai's house was immaculately cleaned. The pool was cleaned and the water gave a blue-ish tinge to everything around it. The pool chairs were neatly arranged and a barbecue was set up. The ambience was perfect to one of the much hyped DHS parties.

As one by one the guests arrived, the music got louder and louder and the party picked up its gusto. The dancing on the floor got wilder as people drunk more, of the expensive alcohol. But Neil Oberoi, the ex-Head Boy of Delhi High School, stood with his girlfriend stuck to his arm, sipping apple juice from his glass. He stood there, away from the dance floor – seemingly uninterested in the hooliganism on display. Instead, he laughed a bit, cracked a few jokes and mostly kept to himself and his girlfriend.

Jai was dancing like a robot with his friends while in the other corner, Rishi and his girlfriend, Shruti were making out, hidden from the view of most.

Jai's one time best-friend and ex-girlfriend, Arzoo giggled her toothy horse like grin every time Jai tried to outdo himself with some act that he thought was funny.

What a goon, she thought. *Almost like a chimpanzee. Good riddance.*

"Watch me bitches," screamed a girl as she took off her shirt and jumped into the pool. Everyone, especially the guys, looked at her as she took off her shoes and shirt. After she had landed in the pool with a loud splash, everyone hooted.

Apart from the important ones, were present the not-so-important ones. Like Jai's personal favourite ass lickers and the wannabe Jais who wanted some *Jainess* transferred into them. Topping the list of them all was Chintan. All his life, he tried walking like Jai, talking like Jai, even acting ape-like like Jai but never managed to get close to the million-dollar grace that Jai Chauhan carried.

As the party went on, the music got louder and more and more people jumped into the pool taking their clothes off. With every splash there was a bigger hoot.

"Do you want to go in?" asked Jai, hoping that Arzoo would've been impressed by now.

"No. Sorry. I'll get a cold if I go" she said and excused herself and stood next to Chintan.

Jai depressed guzzled a few more shots of vodka. And jumped into the pool.

As Arzoo left the party, a few others followed her cue and slowly the terrace of Jai Chauhan was almost empty except for Neil and his girlfriend and Rishi and Shruti.

As Rishi dragged his girlfriend towards the washroom to get some action, a loud noise stopped them in their tracks… There was some kind of commotion going on. Rishi stepped out. He could hear Jai singing on top of his voice inside the pool. He noticed Jai's dad, a noted name in the field of Telecommunications. Next to him was a person who appeared to be a cop in plain clothes. Drunk enough, he was to be talking gibberish to teenagers who were drunk enough to be not trying to understand what he spoke. White flowing mane and a French beard, Jai's dad placed an arm around the cop and guided him towards the elevator. While the glass elevator moved down, Rishi caught a glimpse of Jai's dad sliding his hand into the cop's pocket. And then within moments, both were out of sight.

NINE

The Met department would have predicted turbulence in Vajpai's House No.23 as a destructive tornado. Sasha, Sahana's cousin, had got the results of her Test Series.

She was the daughter of Mr. Arvind Vajpai. The man with a temper of nothing less than a tempest, was screaming at his only child for getting a 91 in Mathematics. Sasha studied in APSN School, Delhi. Not having the prestige of going to her cousin's school didn't bother the frail looking, a little-slow-on-things girl. She didn't resent anything that her cousin had. Rather she pitied her for not having what she had for herself.

Much to their chagrin they both had been born in a family that still lived in the 20th Century when it came to the way their children had to be brought up. Sasha's family was complicated- to say the least actually. Sasha kept on worrying about what her dear mother and respected father would say to her about her marks.

While on the other hand, Sahana avoided thinking about her

family altogether. She would keep herself busy all the time to avoid thinking about it. Whenever something about her family bothered her she slept, ate while reading a book (most of the times), study (rarely), go for a walk (in a park where her friends would be there to greet her to take her for a round of *gol gappas*) and just more sleep.

She rarely thought about how to solve the problems. She'd rather run away from them, far far away. Live alone and be happy. She wished to meet new people who had no clue who she was, so that she could be anything to them.

She thought about every detail of her running away plan from the hell she currently lived in. That she would put her clothes in a backpack, take her money and go to the nearest metro station. Go to the New Delhi Railway Station and take a train from there to Kalka. From there take the bus to Kullu, where she had spent two years of her life. The time spent there, according to her was the best. She kept on daydreaming about what she would do when she got there.

Maybe she would go to her old school and ask for some shelter.

She would convince them that she was an asset and they would let her complete her education and then become a teacher there itself. Or, she thought, a fulltime maid for someone. She would show those people her report cards. They would take pity and maybe admit her into a nearby school.

She kept on coming up with alternatives each time. But that was only when she allowed herself to brood. She made sure that *that* rarely happened.

Mr.Vajpai, Sasha's father, was burning with rage. His daughter had yet again got the same marks in Mathematics as before. He was a man who lost his logical sense when he was angry. This time he was blaming Sasha, but indirectly, blaming Sahana.

"You don't study. *Tumhara dhyan idhar udhur ki cheezon mein zyada jata hai,*" he said with his daughter's paper in his hands. "If Sahana is watching T.V, sit in the other room for god's sakes!" he screamed. "You stay in that room and get hooked on to the television. If she doesn't want to study, why are you not studying? She has already passed her 10th. You haven't!! *Use padhna nahin hai toh tum bhi nahin padhogi?"* He glared at Sahana meaningfully.

"From today onwards you are not studying at all. You will do the housework," he said.

"Seemaaa!" He shouted his wife's name, "*Aaj se yeh ladki ghar ke kaam karegi.*"

Sasha's mother came with hurried steps. She looked at her husband and her daughter. She didn't want to get involved. She knew that her husband's rage was going to go away soon. So she chose to keep quiet.

Sasha was crying. But now that her father had said such words, she became defiant.

"FINE!" she screamed. "I am not going to study. AT ALL! Do what you can."

"*Beta,* stop shouting. *Saare logon ko sunai de raha hoga,*" Sasha's mom said with a serious tone in her voice.

"I don't care!" Sasha screamed again.

"Mummy, where is the broom?" She asked her mother.

"*Beta,* calm down," her mom tried to console her.

"WHERE IS IT?" Sasha now on the verge of exploding screamed louder.

Sahana was watching this drama from one corner of the room. She'd rather not get involved in such unpleasantness. She detested it. She abhorred it. But seeing her cousin go berserk for the first time, she thought that it was time to intervene.

"Okay, okay. *Chacha, chachi aap do minute ke liye jao.* I will explain it to her," Sahana said to the senior Vajpais.

"No need. Let her do what she wants. Two days. That's all it will take her to understand how difficult life is," he said throwing the paper on the floor with disgust.

He walked off from the room and his wife followed.

Sahana quietly closed the door and sat next to Sasha. She hugged Sasha from the side. Sasha cried more profusely now.

"It's okay, *bubah.* It'll be fine. If you just concentrate a little bit more it will be fine." Sahana cajoled her cousin. She hated this part, majorly because she sucked at it. She didn't know what to say at all. She was scared that she might just end up making people cry more.

She frantically thought about what to say next. "*Arre, yaar. Chorr naa.* Get full in the next test okay? Like, don't even make one mistake. Show them that you can do it. Alright?" Sahana said while stroking Sasha's strewn hair.

"I am sick and tired, okay? Why do they always do this? It's a stupid test. Doesn't even count," Sasha said among weeps.

"Baby, they are your parents. They want the best in you. And these tests are there to test how much you've understood the chapter in detail. It's okay. Do better in the next one," she said. Sasha turned away and lay down on the bed. "Yeah...Okay," she mumbled.

"Now, you should get up and start studying. Show them how much you've studied," Sahana encouraged her.

"I need a break," Sasha mumbled. She turned around and asked Sahana, "*Gol gappe khaane hain*?"

"Uhh. Sasha, *dekh, chacha angry hain. Thoda sa padhle.* We

will go after two hours, okay?" Sahana said with hesitation. She didn't want to go. And her intuition was telling her it would be the perfectly wrong time to get out of this house.

"No. I wanna go. NOW!" Sasha got up and started dressing. Sahana sat there with a long look on her face. "If you want to go, then go. I am not coming. I am not abetting you in suicide," she said.

"Fine. Your loss," Sasha said, while putting on her jeans. When Sasha was done, she went out of the room opened the front door and walked out without looking at her parents sitting on the sofa in the room.

Mr. Vajpai got up and rushed to the room where Sahana was sitting.

"What did you tell her to do?!" Mr. Vajpai screamed.

"I told her to study. She wanted a break. I told her not to. She still did. It's not my fault;" she said and turned her face away from the overwhelming man.

"Go after her. God knows what she will do." Sahana stood there for a while. She thought about the prospect of going out. It gave her immense joy to be out of this hell.

"*Theek hai*," she replied in a monotone without facing the red-faced man.

A few minutes later, Sahana and Sasha found themselves sitting in a bare park at one corner of the Mother Dairy outlet that was there nearby. Some old people occupied the only seats available, while what remained of dilapidated swing sets wasn't even worth giving a look. So both the girls decided to stand next to the fence and enjoy their ice cream.

"So tell me. Are there any hot newcomers?" Sasha asked while licking her orange ice-lolly.

"None. I am not kidding. Not even one. It's like all hot guys on this planet are dead. Each one of them is a withered geek or weird-faced," Sahana replied licking the trickle down her hand from the lemon ice-lolly.

"So true. But there must be someone who is moderately good?" Sasha asked shifting her lolly from one hand to the other.

"I don't know, man. Maybe, I didn't notice much. The whole day there are workshops. That's it," Sahana replied.

"Hmm...Good," Sasha said taking a huge bite of her ice-cream.

"Although..." Sahana said.

"What?" Sasha asked with excitement. "Remembered anyone?"

"Arree. Don't worry. He's not hot. He's ok-ok. Kind of do-able. Though he's a writer," Sahana said.

"Ooohh...writer! What book?" Sasha prodded for more information.

"I don't know. I don't remember the book. He told me a week ago," Sahana replied.

"So you've talked to him? Whoa!" Sasha exclaimed.

"He's not a celebrity. Stop getting so excited,"Sahana replied.

"*Chal koi toh hai*," Sasha said, biting her empty stick.

"*Bakwaas na kar*. Let's go," Sahana said, while pulling Sasha by her hand towards their home.

"You should take tuitions," Mr. Vajpai said to his niece.

"Okay. But why?" asked Sahana. What's going on? What new scheme have they thought over? She wondered.

"Because you need them," he replied shifting his weight from one side to another on the huge brown sofa in the living room.

Sahana sat on the opposite side, on the single sofa, thinking. "Can I tell you in an hour about it?" Sahana said, biding for time.

"Okay. An hour," he said with a stern voice.

Sahana got up and straightaway walked into the washroom. She sat on the cold tiled bathroom floor.

She thought about why he was doing it. Why? What possible help can going to tuitions be in this situation? *I guess, they don't want me in the house*, she thought.

She thought about the downside about going to tuitions. She to her own wonder could think of none.

She could only think of the pros. *The reasons I should go to tuitions*, she thought.

a) I get to get out of this hell.

b) I don't have to get involved in the drama.

c) New people.

d) Social life increasing.

e) No need to study in class.

f) Possibility of meeting hot guys.

Ah, hell. I am so going to tuitions!

She opened the latch of the bathroom door. She walked towards the living room. Her uncle was still sitting in the same spot, sipping his evening tea.

"I'll take English tuitions," Sahana said.

"English?" He asked, raising an eyebrow.

"Yes," Sahana replied. She wanted to keep the conversation to the bare minimum.

"Why not Maths?" he asked again.

"My father taught me Math already. I know Mathematics of

Class 12th since Class 9th itself. I don't need it," she replied in a monotone.

"Fine. Where?" he asked.

"I'll find out and tell you," she said and walked out of the room.

"This isn't a very safe idea, you know?" Sahana frowned.

"What's wrong with meeting a guy?" Rishav shrugged his shoulders. He looked around trying to assure Sahana that there was no-one present who could actually pose a threat to either of them.

"It's not about people Sen! It's about my aunt. She comes this way, every Thursday to the temple. Calling me here to meet wasn't the best idea you know." Rishav and Sahana stood close to each other on one side of the main road in Sector 33. As Sahana spoke, she slowly drifted more towards the interiors of the Sector, towards the cold-drinks stalls and *chaat waalas.*

Dressed casually in a brown, wide necked tee and dark jeans, Sahana was perspiring profusely. As the two started walking aimlessly, Rishav tried to engage Sahana in a conversation, before she could raise the much pertinent question regarding the reason for their sudden meet.

"Why on earth are you perspiring so much?" Rishav popped in a question.

"I ran dude. I was already late by fifteen minutes, I was sure you'd be hell annoyed if I delayed you more. So I gobbled up the burger Aunty got for me and ran."

"What excuse did you give?" he asked.

"Umm…I told her that I was going for stationery. Why do you ask?"

"No, just like that. Wanted to know how long you can hang around." The road took a left-turn towards the gigantic main park of that sector. It was evening time and the park was crowded like hell. The dying Sun was like the perfect setting for each and every person present there.

"You waited for fifteen minutes right?" Sahana inquired.

"Not really," he smiled. "You can make that thirty."

"Thirty?! Why? How?" she was surprised.

"Actually, I decided to come fifteen minutes in advance for two reasons…"

"And the reasons being?"

"Um, one I presumed that you'd be on time or maybe before time. So I didn't want to have a situation where I had to keep you waiting and secondly…" he dug his hand into his left pocket. "…and secondly, I thought about arranging for some evening snack you know!" He pulled out two mini-chocolate bars that were a little soggy.

Sahana broke into a short laughter, "You bothered to do that? Stupid you are." She smiled. "Who told you, I liked chocolates?"

"Well, you see… all I saw you doing on your birthday was eating and eating and eating more. And every time, only chocolates! I presumed, it must be on the top of the list of your favourite edibles. Huh?"

"Ah huh dumbass! You got something right for a change," she casually smacked him on the head.

Now that's what friends do, Rishav said to himself. In the meanwhile, Sahana carried on, "…and ooooh! I also like Chinese you know? And McDonalds too....Indian kababs are tasty…"

"Yes yes, you like everything that's edible, you Mother Earth's load. Don't you?" it was perhaps the most casual sentences Rishav could have ever spoken in his life. However, it warranted a not-so-casual response.

"Uh, I detest fat jokes. Okay?" she spoke with an absolute straight face.

"You aren't fat, so why should you take this personally?

"Because I just did so, dude." She seemed visibly annoyed.

"Point noted, but can we get over with the sappy stuff now?" he asked innocently.

"Sappy?"

Rishav shook the two mini-bars in front of her eyes.

"Oh that..." she said. "...sure, thanks!"

And they started dirtying their hands and faces. It took Rishav seconds to get done with his bar but it seemed Sahana relished every inch of it.

"You have a tissue?" she asked.

"No. But I have a handkerchief," he slid his hand inside his jeans pockets to get it out.

"No no, not handkerchiefs, they aren't hygienic!"

Rishav made an expression that was hard to miss, "What?"

"Arre, they aren't hygienic and it applies to everyone, not you in specific... dumbo!"

"Oh!" he managed to calm down a bit.

"So you don't have a tissue eh?" she confirmed again.

"Apparently not, but you can surely use my jeans to wipe the chocolate. It'll go for laundry anyway." Rishav encouraged her by wiping his own hands first.

"Oh and also..." he began.

"Huh?"

"…also, try and keep it restricted to your hands only. There's chocolate all over your face too and it wouldn't be too good for people to see you wiping you face on my legs you know?" he tried hard to be funny.

"Rishav Sen, did anyone ever point out that your jokes make no-sense at all? And are pretty lame?"

"Now, that was blunt!" Rishav replied.

"Do get used to it, as you'll be in for more…" she flashed her trademark lopsided grin.

And while Rishav searched for an apt reply, Sahana preempted his move and followed it with another snide remark, "your hair, you kind of look dorky in it. Do push it back when you are around me?"

"Really?" he confirmed.

"Yeah, but again it's a personal choice. If you *want* to, that is. Otherwise, I'd just avoid looking at your face." She said.

"Oh so you'll be talking to me looking straight at my chest, will you now? Now I wonder if I ever did the same when ugly chicks came in front of me, I'd be mauled!" he laughed at his own joke.

"Dude…!" she exclaimed.

"What?"

"…lame again!" she smiled and moved her head in a circular motion.

"Damnit!" Rishav replied.

As they completed an entire round of the park's perimeter, Sahana got reminded of the question she was supposed to ask in the first place. "Why did we meet today?"

"Oh, actually tomorrow is my dog, Ruffle's birthday. I am kind of celebrating it on my own. Join me for lunch would you?" Rishav made up something obscure.

"You celebrate your dog's birthday?"

Rishav nodded.

"What do I tell my aunt? Why was I late?" she inquired.

"Tell her you had some stay-back shit. She'll believe you."

"What if I get caught?" Came another question.

"Seriously dudette, we spent twenty-five minutes together at a place barely five hundred meters away from your place. What else can be riskier than this?" Rishav tried analyzing the thing logically.

"That's true, but isn't the risk too much?"

"Ask your friend Vanya, it's a basic principle – risk involves probability of huge profits. So shall I count you in my guest list?"

"You have a guest list too?" she was intrigued.

"Yes, as of now the list just has the names of two people, you know. And I doubt it whether they'll be further additions."

"And the two people being?"

"Rishav Sen and Sahana Vajpai," he stopped to notice her reaction to this carefully. She had a straight face initially, as though she hadn't got what he had said completely. And then the expression changed to that of amusement. "Aren't the two enough?" Rishav added,

"Of course they are," Sahana concurred.

"So would you be there with me tomorrow, after school?" he was persistent.

"Why do we ask when we already know what the answer is?" said Sahana.

"Why do we not tell when we know how much our answer means to the person?" Rishav replied.

"Because my friend, some things in life are better left to be understood," a smile lit up Sahana's face.

Rishav reciprocated. "I will see you in school tomorrow and then after school too," he said.

"You know my decision?"

Rishav nodded.

"Then you know right," she looked at him for a second or so and then started walking again.

While Sahana headed back home, she briefly went through the first few texts she had exchanged with Rishav. One of them read:

'I am allergic to animals. Dogs in specific. Can't stand one. Never ever had a pet and neither will have one. – sent by Rishav.'

There was a certain experience of buoyancy at that point of time for Sahana. *He tries too hard*...she thought.

TEN

"We call him *Aam-chutiya*!" Hardik whispered into Jai's ear, who started chuckling the moment he heard the name. "He likes nibbling on Mangoes and *chut* and he is ordinary, hence, *aam-chutiya!*" Hardik explained on a louder note, much to the annoyance of the Accountancy teacher.

A better part of Siddhant's school days were spent having people poke fun at him. Be it his shabby Hindi pronunciation or his diet or his diction – the 'popular' ones would ensure that Siddhant was at the receiving end of all their taunts. And his fault?

He just didn't cede to their superficiality. He didn't lick their asses like other *wannabes* did.

"He knows you guys call him this?" Jai asked.

"Yeah man, he does," Hardik replied. "Despite that, he's such a loser man, he doesn't protest!"

"Ha ha ha..!" Jai laughed. He looked at Siddhant who was

taking down notes with a lot of intent. It was as though his whole life depended on those twenty minutes spent inside class, taking notes. Jai felt a tad sad for him. Two years and no recognition would have been terrible, he thought. Personally, Jai had started mixing with the right kinds and laying the right foundation for becoming the Head Boy, ever since he was in Class IX. Networking and diplomacy was something Jai's dad had taught him ever since birth.

"Sleep with the maid if needed, but ensure that at the end of it you have gained something considerable!" Jai's dad had told him this when Jai had gone to find out whether being manipulative was unethical.

"Ethics, young man..." Jai's dad had broken into a burst of laughter when he heard Jai's question. "...ethics and success don't walk on the same road Son, you will realize that. You are meant for big things, so don't let tiny people come your way." Jai had taken these words with considerable amounts of seriousness and it was visible in the way he dealt with people in school. He wasn't the types to go out of the way to help someone in need, he would just appear to be helping that person or maybe he would first try to find out how his act would benefit his reputation and after all these considerations would he extend his helping hand. Jai's principles seldom worked beyond the definitions of a ledger, trial balance and a balance sheet...everything had a direct bearing on his goodwill. And his job was to keep it enhanced as much as he could.

"Let's go and heckle him," Hardik suggested.

"*Nahi yaar*, leave it. He is a *chut* anyway, why bother?" Jai replied with his usual calmness that accompanied his stupid logic.

"You wait and watch, let me do it..." Hardik got up to move closer to Siddhant. A whack on the head with his notebook would be enough. And the Accountancy teacher wouldn't really do anything to His Highness Jai's friend. And this in fact gave Hardik a lot of encouragement to do silly stuff which he would not have done otherwise.

"I told you, *sit*!" Jai raised his voice. The bark was enough to remind the class of the royalty's presence within their walls. Despite it being a clear cut disturbance, the teacher just looked at Jai with *I-know-you-did-it-again* expression and carried on with her teaching.

"Bitch, I told you not to!" Jai scowled.

"Sorry maaaan! I didn't know you'd get so peeved so quickly?"

"Then know so! I am not in my best of mood these days, so understand!" Jai spoke with authority.

"What happened man? Something serious?" Hardik replied.

"You know it," Jai said. "It's that Sen-guy! He's making me jittery."

"What about him?" Hardik was inquisitive.

"They way he ass-licks people around, his fuckin' charm and his sugar-coated comments. It's making all the teachers go gaga over him. Asshole he is man, I'll bloody fuck him if he pips me to the Head Boy's post!"

"Head Boy? That pimp is applying for Head Boy?" Hardik's jaw dropped, metaphorically, not literally.

"Yeah he is and I am pretty sure that he will end up getting it despite my candidature."

"No *re*, that's not possible dude! You are *Jai Chauhan*, the poster boy of DHS, how can *anyone* replace you overnight?" there came a spontaneous response.

"But there must be some way of getting that bitch down? Find dirt man, go find dirt on him!" Jai ordered.

"Dirt? What kind of dirt do you want on him?"

"Any will do. His weakness, it can be a person or a trait or anything for that matter. Something that'll make him cut a sorry figure. You find that out and then we can nail his not *so* holy image in front of Veenu." Jai spoke as Hardik nodded.

His Highness had just put one of his subjects on a daunting mission. A lot was at stake for Jai and this mission was perhaps very crucial to ensure that if there was one winner at the end of it all, it would be Jai!

"Don't you dare talk to me now!" Sahana snapped as she pushed the chair back in the library with a lot of noise. Some heads turned to see the commotion; the Library in-charge sent a frosty glare from behind the layers of books crowding her table.

Sahana got up to vacate the seat she was occupying; a taken aback Rishav Sen, mustered a lot of courage and mumbled, "What now?"

"You know *shit* about me!" Sahana hissed. "And right now, you are just being a presumptuous dickhead," she said.

Rishav scratched the back of his head before meekly submitting his response, "Mind the language woman..." "...how on Earth am I supposed to know that calling you by the name of an Indian revolutionary might just piss you off?"

"It just did and *seriously* now, don't talk to me!" She turned her back on him and stormed towards another seat across the gigantic Library of Delhi High School.

Rishav sat there for a few seconds, trying to come to terms with the intensity of what just struck him. After all the drama of creating a non-existent dog's birthday, fixing up a date, making Sahana make excuses – he calls her by the name of a weird Indian freedom fighter and BAM! There she goes, all mad at him. By the time Rishav had steadied his nerves, Sahana was at the far corner of the hall checking out the magazine section. *I got this date after a lot of effort*, Rishav thought. *And I won't screw it up*, he added. So he gathered the balls to walk up and tried not to sport a puppy dog face. He knew how repulsed Sahana would get had he tried the fake antics of making cute-innocent-puppy dog apologetic expressions. Trying to be normal, he approached Sahana; who on seeing him turned around and walked straight back to her seat. Rishav tailed her as he felt the gaze of a number of eyeballs following his actions.

He sat down right next to Sahana, much to her annoyance. "I am sorry?" he said.

"Was that a question?" She asked.

"Not really. Just that I didn't intend any harm and besides I wasn't aware that that name would affect you so badly," he spoke in a lowered voice.

Sahana looked at him, visibly pissed as she formed her reply. "Whatever," she said.

Whatever? Rishav said to himself. *Damn these women,* he thought.

Sahana couldn't really care less about a person who when repeatedly being warned about something didn't listen. Yes, it was true that she had once made a mention of how Rishav should judge from her response and should stop and see whether the joke is being taken sportingly by her or not, rather than continue with his incessant blabbering. She was the type who'd rather stay away from such people.

But, on the contrary, Rishav cared of course. He did. And right now what mattered was the apology to be accepted. Why?

For Rishav it was *need* and Sahana saw that to be his ulterior motive. That day was supposed to be their first unofficial date and being the despo he was, he badly hoped that Sahana would not let this bizarre incident ruin his much worked out plan, but to his chagrin – she kind of had already got a feel of how much he wanted the day to work out. She was smarter than what Rishav perceived her to be. And not being around many intelligent girls, numbed Rishav's sense of judgment of whether the girl in front of him was a step ahead of him or not.

Sahana came under the category of girls who didn't like guys who tried too hard. And it would take time for Rishav to realize that - and that too, the hard way. And according to her, their date now stood *officially cancelled.* The news had a bad effect on Rishav. With a sunken heart, he insisted that Sahana reconsider her stand. It was a stupid incident after all but she felt otherwise. *He better get used to it*, she thought.

And the day passed with nothing much as Rishav decided to just let it go. He had apologized and there wasn't much that he could do. Maybe he didn't know why that name might have offended her, but then to his defense – how would he if she never shared? For the first time, Rishav got the taste of a colourless day. And the missing colour was Sahana who refused to talk to him, his feelings for her were getting stronger – something that he realized quicker than he should have.

ELEVEN

Jai Chauhan appeared to be the typical villain, like in every story but there existed a good-side to him that Rishav badly wanted to discover.

Situations had made Jai what he was. He was not the one who would express love or emotions to people because he had been taught to remain calm, composed and focused towards the task at hand at all times in life – to be successful in every situation that faced him. This was something that he learnt from his father apart from the glorious pieces of advice and anecdotes that the senior Chauhan often shared with him. But it was actually the missing love of a separated mother that made him realize that human emotions were worthless or as he called them – *a bag of crap that pulls you back!*

He walked towards the Audio-Visual Room with his usual long strides, covering as much ground as possible. On reaching the room, he knocked on the door twice. Without any further wait, he pulled the door towards himself and slipped into the room.

A little away from the Audio-Visual Room, Muskaan Kaur accompanied by some of her most trusted aides waited outside Bindu Kalsi's office. They had sought an appointment with the Principal and since it was Muskaan, an appointment was more of a formality.

The buzzer went off, indicating that Kalsi was ready to meet them. Muskaan was the first to pop her head in, "May we come in ma'am?" she spoke in a tone that was loud enough to make Kalsi lift her eyes up from the circular she was reading.

Kalsi smiled, "Muskaan, please come in..."

Muskaan walked in first, closely followed by her two colleagues. Kalsi folded the circular and put it inside her drawer. "What brings you here?" She asked.

"Ma'am, my colleagues and I intend to begin work for *Socialact Wave* as soon as possible," Muskaan replied.

"*Socialact Wave?* So early? Isn't it a good couple of months away already?" Kalsi's glasses rested on the tip of her nose. She read each face present in the room carefully through the deep shades of kajal that underlined her eyes.

Socialact Club was one of the most popular clubs around in Delhi High School. Its membership was only restricted to the popular ones who had fathers with heavy pockets. The entrance criteria was as simple as it could get – be cool, hang around with the right kinds, talk of big stuff and whollah, you are in! Muskaan Kaur and her colleagues (the couple of them who were present in the room) were jointly responsible for running the club and making it what it was; with a little bit of luck and a whole lot of contacts! And Socialact Wave was the Inter-School music fest that was held every year under the banner of the Socialact Club. It was one of those events which witnessed a lot of money splurging, shady sponsorship deals, consumption of alcohol by minors and usual murk expected in a high-society co-ed school in the suburbs of Delhi.

"It's been five years since we've had it outside on a grand scale, we intend to do so this time," said Muskaan convincingly.

"Outside?" Kalsi asked.

"By outside, I mean outside the Auditorium. In the school ground preferably. Five years is a long wait and we do not intend to wait any longer." The other two people present in the room shook their heads in support of what Muskaan just said as though their life depended on Socialact Wave going outdoors.

Kalsi remained silent for a while till she herself broke the silence, "You do know Muskaan and let me mince no words, we would be requiring triple the funds for organizing such an event on a grand scale. Where would you gather such huge amounts of money?"

"Sponsorship…" Muskaan began. Bindu Kalsi for the first time got visibly impatient, "What sponsorship are you talking about? The sponsors previous year had paid one-third of what they'd be expected to pay this year and every time we can't expect overwhelming support can we?"

"Yes we can," Muskaan said. "We have internal support this time and with your permission we can convert that into an overwhelming support system."

"What do you imply?" Kalsi took off her specs and rubbed her temple.

"Compulsory sponsorship from students will really help the cause…"

"Are you out of your mind Muskaan? We are answerable to the parents!" Kalsi raised her voice.

"Tch tch…Bindu, I agree we *are* answerable to the parents but not when the Parents' Association representative is on our side," a smile lit Muskaan's face.

Kalsi raised her eyebrows in inquisitiveness.

"Yes, you heard it right. Veer Chauhan is ready to support our demand for compulsory donations from students. And if he does so, I doubt it whether parents would disagree. Jolly old Veer," Muskaan smirked.

"Veer Chauhan...? You mean Jai's father?" Kalsi replied.

"Yes and he has also agreed to make 75% payment for the setup costs of the entire function's infrastructure with the help of his Telecom Service Providing firm."

"That is interesting, how did you convince him?"

"It was simple, Socialact Wave this year shall be the grandest Wave ever and it shall so happen under your leadership. Isn't that a proud occasion?" Muskaan ranted.

Bindu Kalsi's chest puffed up with pride, "Yes indeed."

"Veer Chauhan has agreed to provide unconditional help in the form of cash and kind but in return all we need to do is tweak the rules a bit." Muskaan paused. There was silence all around.

"...Jai Chauhan needs to be made Secretary of Socialact Club despite not being of the permitted class and..." she spoke in a low tone.

"And...?" Kalsi moved a little forward.

Muskaan took in a deep breath, "...and Jai also has to be given first choice preference when the Council is nominated and the Head Boy is selected."

Kalsi looked at her in disbelief, so did the accompanying teachers who had no inkling of what Muskaan had to say.

Muskaan got up from her seat, Kalsi still hadn't spoken a word. "We need to decide on this Bindu," she said. "...we need to decide on it soon. You are on the path to becoming the greatest Principal in the history of DHS and all that separates you from that tag is a petty post that needs to be given to a boy whose father....erm, whose father is perhaps one of the most generous people you'll ever come across. And he doesn't really demand much in return and it's nothing that you *can't* provide." Muskaan curtly nodded as she rounded off her sentence and got ready to leave.

Bindu Kalsi pushed herself back on her reclining chair. In a contemplative mood, she thought of all that Muskaan had said. Some things made sense while others still remained ambiguous in her head. On one side she had her principles while on the other side she had instant success. She lifted her intercom and dialed for her secretary. A couple of rings later, the secretary was on the line.

"Connect me to the Chairman," Kalsi said and put the receiver down. She looked at Muskaan and gave a semi affirmative nod.

Though unspoken, Muskaan knew word-to-word what Bindu Kalsi's nod suggested. She was a happy woman and why not!

TWELVE

Who cares about school events like special assemblies, academic workshops, usual festival oriented occasions, it's time for Socialact Wave.

This was perhaps the most overused line in the build up to Socialact Wave. Delhi High School seemed to have been engulfed by the father of all waves of activity. Students, teachers, office staff and employees alike – everyone was seen where they were *not* supposed to be seen. Teachers were no longer within the walls of their Staff Room sipping their hot cups of tea, instead were seen doing a variety of tasks that included designing contingency plans, assisting the Heads with the invite list, coordinating with the Office Administration and all. Students who never really enjoyed the comforts of their classroom finally got a chance to smell the fresh air again – the air of the corridors. Varying in shapes and sizes, students could be seen all over the corridors. Most were accompanied by a Socialact Club member, who'd be appearing to be in a lot of work yet not be in any. The students were involved in work that ranged from designing posters to helping in transferring decoration items from one end of the school to another. Other students including His Highness Jai Chauhan went about ordering people, flaunting his influence and doing things that would be included under the broad sub-heading as *chutiyapanti.*

Every year, Socialact Wave was an event that was highly anticipated and people would actually look forward to it due to its tremendous glamour quotient. Unlimited caffeinated drinks and food to those who paid up sponsorship money was an incentive. And since, sponsorships were compulsory that year, *everyone* was entitled to the food and beverage. Crisp circulars had ensured that all students, willing or unwillingly had to pay up four hundred rupees towards sponsorship for Socialact Wave. Besides, there were separate forms for the rich Daddies like that of Jai who'd sponsor the entire banner that was being put up. And it'd be unrealistic to say that students couldn't really find good sponsors, a famous liquor brand named *Royal Hag* was ready to pay up to twenty five lakhs but much to the disappointment of many – they were refused by the image conscious Bindu Kalsi.

The program for Socialact Wave included performances by Western music bands from twenty schools in and around the National Capital Region. Apart from that there was usually one professional band that would play some of its suckiest songs for exorbitant prices. Follow it up with a boring speech from the Chairman and an encore performance by the previous year's school band- that was Socialact Wave for you. But, somehow amidst the head-banging, foot-tapping and screaming, lay tremendous interest that had been generated over the years in favour of the event. Be it the food, the official beverage which included Pepsi or the unofficial one which included bottles of Vodka within the cisterns inside the bathroom, Wave had unparalleled acceptance all over the school.

Veer Chauhan scribbled something on a form that seemed like his signature. "Thank you for this opportunity Bindu," he said. He lifted the glass of water lying right in front of him and took a few sips.

"Anytime Veer, anytime," Bindu Kalsi said. "It's really kind of you to be generous enough to contribute towards the school's progress. Parents like you are highly appreciated."

"It's as much my school as it is yours," Veer Chauhan replied.

Bindu Kalsi coughed a bit. She didn't want to share anything, let alone her Kingdom.

"Yes, yes…" she superficially said.

"So, once this token amount is encashed, do I expect some good news regarding my son?" Mr. Chauhan said trying to be humble and in a way insulting the six zeros that had been put next to the digit 15 on the cheque that he had just signed.

"We are definitely trying to work things out," Kalsi said. "We will see what can be done in the best interests of your son and the school." Diplomacy was being used at its best no matter how sore it sounded to the ears.

"You do know Bindu that my son's interests lay in the interest of the school," he chuckled.

Late to catch his sense of humour, Bindu Kalsi laughed for the sake of laughing.

"Is there anything else I could do for you?" Mr. Chauhan asked.

"No, your help is tremendous. Thank you for that."

"Then I shall take your leave," a firm shake of hand and Jai Chauhan's Super dad was gone.

"Socialact Wave, add all the murk around you and then triple it – you'll still not manage to add up to the dirt this event brings to our school," Siddhant Dalvi spoke in a circumspective tone.

Rishav nodded. "Is it true that it's going outdoors after five years? Is it that big a deal?" he asked.

"Yes it is, my friend. A lot of excess money enters the school through events such as these. It's very important."

"Hmm.... does anyone even bother to monitor these funds? Seriously I heard that brands like the *Royal Hag* were willing to pay for sponsorship. What's left of an educational institution these days?"

"Nothing really," Siddhant said as he knocked on the door of Ms. Veenu Sharma. "Come in," the call came from inside.

Siddhant entered with Rishav closely following him.

"Good morning ma'am," Rishav and Siddhant said in unison.

"Morning, morning," Ms. Sharma smiled.

"Ma'am, the sponsorship amounts," Siddhant handed over a cheque.

"How much is it?" she asked.

"Ten thousand," he replied.

"Ah hmmmmm....so what are your plans?" she asked out of nowhere.

"Erm ma'am, are you asking me?" Siddhant asked.

"To both of you, heheheheee..." she laughed unnecessarily.

"Oh, ma'am, well...um, plans regarding?" Rishav asked.

"Plans regarding what you want to do for the school. Council interviews next week," she said.

"Council interviews? Really ma'am?" Siddhant asked.

"Yes," Veenu nodded. "We will be giving out the forms shortly.

It's going to be a couple of days before Socialact Wave."

"I see," Rishav said. "Ma'am is there any criteria to apply? New students too can, can't they? For the top posts?"

"Yes, yes they can. You have a lot of backing from teachers and what's your name again?" She answered Rishav first and then looked at Siddhant trying hard to recollect his name.

"Siddhant, ma'am. Siddhant Dalvi," he seemed slightly offended.

"Yes yes, Siddhant. What do you want to do? I haven't really seen you much. How long have you been here?"

"3 years ma'am," he said proudly.

"I see, but your contribution has been useless," there was bluntness everywhere.

"Okay ma'am," Siddhant replied. "...but I do intend to apply for the Council as I feel that I have had considerable contributions to talk about," he added.

"You feel? Huh!" she scoffed.

"I know ma'am," he replied.

"*Accha accha,* I am busy now, wait outside – I need to have a word with Rishav," Ms. Sharma seemed to have got reminded of her busy schedule all of a sudden.

Siddhant nodded politely, wished her, turned around and left the cabin.

"What's with this Sahana girl?" Veenu asked.

"Ma'am, who?" Rishav was flustered.

"This girl called Sahana Vajpai, I've noticed both of you hanging out a lot lately. Your girlfriend?"

"No, not at all ma'am. Just a friend," he maintained his calm.

"I have got reports of seeing you guys at places, avoid okay? I see you as a potential Head Boy candidate this year."

"Right ma'am. I am glad you could share this with me," he mumbled.

"I have other news too, but ensure to keep it to you." She lowered her voice.

"What ma'am?"

"Jai's dad has got a deal done in order to make him the Head Boy, you have very stiff competition," a concerned Veenu Sharma spoke.

"And why do you tell me this?" he was inquisitive.

"Because, I don't like this Jai guy. He's a person of double standards and I don't like this two-faced Muskaan either. I am just warning you, motherly advice. Be careful of what you are getting yourself into." She sounded stern till the point a lot of bitterness took over.

"Muskaan ma'am seemed very sweet..." Rishav began and he was quickly interrupted.

"She seems sweet to everyone. Just be careful okay?"

"Okay," he nodded unknowing of what to do.

"Good," she smiled again, opened her drawer and took out a Kitkat.

"Take this," she said. "....have it yourself and *don't* share it with Sahana, hehehhehe...!" her trademark laugh followed.

"Ha ha, thank you ma'am." Rishav said as he accepted the small bar of chocolate without a complaint.

THIRTEEN

'*Lunch today?'* Rishav scribbled on a piece of paper, stuffed it inside the cap of his blue Trimax gel pen and casually dropped it on Sahana's desk as he walked past it.

Sahana who was deeply engrossed in her talks failed to respond to Rishav's futile attempt. To make it look less obvious, Rishav went straight down to the far end of the classroom and sat besides Tarun Saini who was in one of his hormone drives.

"Pee-shove Hen," Tarun exclaimed on seeing him.

"Hey!" Rishav said as he positioned himself to get an unhindered view of Sahana. She was *yet* to turn around and spot the lonely pen cap lying on her desk. *Urgh,* Rishav scowled in his head.

In the meanwhile, Tarun Saini had started muttering stuff like how pressurized the modern youth was. To top that, he composed an impromptu song and started humming it under his breath, *Pressure, pressure everywhere – no pressure when we shit! We shall bust pressure with our busty chests and this idea is a HIT!*

Saini's insanity added to an anxious Rishav's woes. It had been a good fifteen minutes or so, since he had left that well-disguised note and Sahana seemed least interested.

Rishav looked at the heavens, *kill me O' Lord!* Tarun took cue and started, *Kill me, thrill me, kiss me but don't forget to fuck me, ah huh ah huh...*

Irritated, annoyed and anxious – Rishav got up. He walked upto Sahana and stood beside her for a few seconds. She failed to acknowledge his presence. He lifted the pen cap and shook it violently in front of Sahana's eyes and in the process disturbed her and broke her flow of conversation in which she was vaguely explaining the nuances of mountain climbing.

"Uff! What the hell are you doing?! Get away!" she screamed.

"I am bringing to your notice that this pen cap has been lying on your desk for the past *fifteen minutes*!" Rishav exclaimed.

"So?" she replied.

"So, see what it's about!"

"Get lost, I am busy. I will see it later," she was sharp and merciless in her tone of reply.

"Just see it atleast?" Rishav's tone on the contrary, reflected desperation.

"Can't you get it once?" Sahana sounded cross. "I don't *want* to, now go...!"

"Why you getting pissed *yaar*?" Rishav asked. "I just wanted you to see what was inside," he mumbled.

Her brows burrowed in a frown, she made an expression reflecting distaste and disgust and turned to face her friend again.

Rishav stood there for a moment or two, before dragging

himself back to where Tarun Saini sat.

"Crack some of your jokes man!" He said, quite frustrated.

It was one of those moments when anyone would be dying to say, *oh dear earth dig a hole and bury me inside it.*

Saini's funny jokes didn't sound funny anymore and with no other alternatives left, Rishav placed his head on the desk and tried to fall asleep when something terribly hard struck him on the head with force.

He got up startled; he saw a pen-cap lying next to him on the floor.

He lifted it and took out the crumbled piece of paper. There was a sense of excitement, anticipating what could be Sahana's reply. And much to his dismay, the note read: *NO.*

What the hell! He kicked himself. Now that was the second time, he was being refused directly or indirectly. *Enough is enough*, he thought.

The queerness of humans is that there's a lot of disparity between what one thinks and how his actions follow up his thoughts. And so was the same, in case of Rishav.

"You wanted dirt, I have dirt!" Hardik exclaimed proudly.

Jai sat in his zone at the far end of the school ground. He was surrounded by two-three of his other ass lickers. Stubbles and disheveled hair, the royalty wasn't really at his best that day. He looked at Hardik for a few seconds. His icy cold stare read the twitching of every facial muscle of Hardik whilst he spoke. Jai had his arms folded and legs crossed, "What's the dirt bitch?" he asked.

"A girl," Hardik replied.

People around Jai started laughing.

"A girl?" Jai mocked Hardik's incoherent tone.

"Yes, Sahana. Sahana Vajpai."

"Sahana?" there was a drastic change in Jai's expressions. "*That* Sahana?" he reconfirmed.

"Yes dude. *That* Sahana."

"Fuck!" Jai got up, unnerving his pals in the process. "This is fucking insane man, now I get to get back at *both* of them!" he laughed.

"Don't you have history with her?" Hardik asked.

"Yes I do, she was the one who beat me blue with her water bottle in the junior classes when I accidentally called her a stale tomato!" Jai scratched his head. "And then, a few years later, she tried to report me to Madhuri for misusing my powers as the class monitor. Although Madhuri ma'am didn't do anything to me, but I still have some resentment towards that bitch!"

"Well then…" Hardik said. "…she's the bitch Rishav is after. Seen them loads together you know. Library, canteen, games periods, everywhere they'll be seen together. It's the Rishav-Sahana show." He added.

"Have they been seen doing any hanky panky?" Jai started moving up and down with people following him as he did that. "Stop following me *bhenchods*," he shouted.

"No hanky panky, Rishav has played it safe. He doesn't want to screw up his reputation."

"Hmm… I see. So you imply that if I intimidate the chick, the cock will do something unsavoury?" he deliberately said *cock,* much to the delight of his mates.

"I guess as much," Hardik said.

"Then we shall do that, we shall do something to unsettle

Sahana and provoke that *Bengali* bitch."

"As you say, what do we have to do?"

"I will call you in the evening and tell you what needs to be done, it's of utmost important that we do this. And that too, successfully," Jai thumped his fist on his shoulder.

Too excited about provoking Rishav, Jai forgot that he was taking on the very girl who turned him into a state in which even his mom failed to recognize him!

FOURTEEN

Rishav had given up trying to make things work and arrange for a lunch with Sahana on a sooner date. Everytime, she came in front him, he wanted to have a chance to talk to her about "stuff." But despite his repeated tries, it didn't work. Not much worked when it came to Sahana, really!

He looked down at his watch and saw that it was almost two. He was already out of class. *I am not going back*, he said to himself. *Even if it means not seeing her go and not seeing her for two days*, he thought.

He went to the canteen, hung out with some random people and headed towards the exit, after that. He walked slowly with the scorching sun on his back. He looked up and saw a lonely figure standing there. Black bag, blue stripes on it – a girl. *Is that Sahana?* He thought. Now, the last thing he wanted was to get his hopes up and running unnecessarily.

He reached the gate, walking slowly because there was a little glimmer of hope inside him. He looked at the girl, carefully from the back. *Yes it was* Sahana!

Act cool, act cool Rishav, he told himself.

"Hey," he said in a not so enthusiastic though not too mellow manner. She smiled. "How come you're here? Don't you go by bus?" he asked.

"Yeah, missed my bus," she replied.

"So how do you plan to go then?"

"I have no friggin' clue!" she exclaimed.

"Rickshaw?" Rishav asked.

"Need money for that. And if I had it, wouldn't I have been at home by now?" she did her little thing with the eyes.

"Okay, then," he replied to that. "You can take the money from me. Return it to me later," he added laying emphasis on the last part.

She hesitated, shifting from one foot to another. "I can't, because if I go home now, they'd scold me for missing my bus." "And if I go home and make an excuse of a stay-back, then they'll scold me for not informing them before hand!"

"Call them from the Reception area," Rishav suggested.

"Yeah," she said still thinking. "Okay, let's go to the Reception then," she said.

He was surprised that she actually let him come with her.

"Cool," he said in a state of subdued excitement.

She walked with a haste he hadn't seen before.

"So your aunt and uncle are really strict, huh?" he asked trying to talk while they ran and walked at the same time.

"Strict would be an understatement," she replied.

"Oh, okay!" he said. He wanted to ask a lot of questions but figured that it'd be just too rude to be all probing, so he kept silent.

"You've been in this school all along?" he asked.

"No, I was also in DAV Shimla," she replied.

"Ohh, I just *love* that place. I lived there for a year or a little more."

"You did? Then how come we never banged into each other then?" she asked for the sake of it. As though it in an afterthought, she added, "I was five years old then. I don't think we'd even remember even if we did bang into each other."

"I would've," he said innocently.

They reached the Reception and she put on her – *I'm a little troubled girl, help me* face.

The receptionist, seeing her face, melted and let her make the phone call. After long, drawn out explanations and persuasive statements, Sahana hung up. With a long face, she walked towards Rishav.

"So?" he asked. "What did she say?" he added.

"Well, I told her that I had a stay-back and that I had forgotten to inform her," she felt silent.

"And…?"

"And, she is kinda cross at me but I think I might manage it, if my uncle doesn't get all aggressive and stuff. I told her I'd be back in an hour, just to be convincing."

"Hmmm…" Rishav nodded. "You must be hungry," he said. "So am I…!" he followed it up, not giving Sahana, a moment to reply.

"What do you mean?" she asked.

"Well, there's a McD outlet close by, want to go and grab a bite?" for the first time what he said wasn't aimed at creating situations for a lunch. Things just happened and they had reached a situation where a lunch was the most apparent thing.

"Umm...I don't know really. I honestly don't want be spotted; I'll be in deep shit if I do. You go ahead," she said.

"Sahana, trust me. It'll be fine, we can take an auto. You know? The ones with covered sides, it'll conceal you."

She stood there for a while, thinking. *Oh what the hell! I am going,* she said to herself.

Fifteen minutes later, they were looking up at the menu at the back of the counter, in the restaurant of McDonald's.

"I'll go with a McAloo," she said with childlike enthusiasm.

Rishav looked at her and smiled, "And I thought you weren't interested in lunch."

"Well, it's Mcd's. Every child's dream land, you know," she said.

Rishav smiled again, "And you are a child. I get it. McAloo for me too, then," he said.

"Vegetarian? Seriously? Aren't you like a crazy non-vegetarian?" she asked.

"Well, I feel like McAloo. So why can't I? I have never tried it before. Today, my intuition tells me is the perfect day," Rishav said.

"As you wish, order a small fries and a regular Coke that we'll share okay?" she said.

"Why not separate?" he countered.

"I can't drink the whole thing. I'll waste it. Do as I say. I am gonna wait outside."

"Here you go," he said, five minutes later, as he handed Sahana her McAloo burger.

"Coke?" she asked.

"Here you go," he handed her the Coke.

She took a sip and handed it back to him.

"So how are you gonna eat with both your hands occupied?" she laughed.

"I guess you'll have to hold the Coke while I eat my burger," he thrust the Coke in her hand.

"Don't push it. I am clumsy. I might just drop it," she said jokingly.

Rishav finished his burger in three bites.

"Talk about animalistic," she commented as she stared at him crushing the burger's wrapper into a ball and putting it back into the brown paper bag.

"What?" Rishav asked after he had swallowed everything.

"Three bites and it's finished," Sahana said while slowly eating her burger.

"Hello! I was hungry okay? And that's how guys eat. They have big appetites," he said defensively.

"Yeah. You're right. That's how they eat. Like primeval animals. True," Sahana said as she started walking towards their auto.

"Oh please," Rishav said, afraid if he became too offensive she would get even more offensive.

"Now finish the Coke. I will finish the fries," Sahana ordered as they stood next to the auto.

"I want the fries too. I am still hungry," Rishav said.

"No. I want the fries. You eat my burger," Sahana said.

"Oh God, fine. Give it to me," Rishav snatched the burger out of Sahana's hands before she could take another bite.

"Bitch!" Sahana said as she snatched the fries out of his hand.

"Let's go," he ordered.

"Okay. I have to get back anyway," Sahana agreed.

They sat in the auto. A silence crept up between them. Rishav was not restless to say something for the first time. He was content.

Sahana stopped the auto before the main gate of 34.

"Bye," she said as she got off from the auto.

Rishav smiled and waved as the auto sped off towards his home.

FIFTEEN

"Rishav Sen, right?" Kalsi asked with half smile lighting up her oblate spheroid face.

"Yes ma'am," Rishav replied with all sincerity.

"Take a seat," she pointed towards the chair in front of her.

Rishav took the support of the armrests to sit down comfortably; he didn't want a situation where he would miss the chair and land on the floor with a thud. He looked up and saw the faces that surrounded Bindu Kalsi, apprehensively.

There was Veenu Sharma, glowing more than what the moon would on any given night. There was Neeti Chopra who wore a sari that was gloomier than her expression. There was the Eco teacher who gave Rishav, nightmares of his first interview and megalomaniac Physics H.O.D. who seemed to be interested in almost everything that happened in the school.

"Nice recommendations Rishav, hehehee…!" Veenu broke the silence.

Her closing laughter killed all the nervous tension present inside the room. Rishav nodded, slightly more confident than what he was when he first entered the room. He could feel the beads of sweat that were trickling down his neck and back.

"You have applied for?" Neeti Chopra questioned, also adjusting her dull sari while she did so.

"Head Boy ma'am!"

"What have you done for the school?" Bindu sounded sepulchral.

"Since, I am a new student, my contributions have been limited but besides that in my limited opportunity and time, I have done the following..." Rishav listed down all his contributions and achievements over the brief period he had spent in DHS.

"I see, I see..." Kalsi acknowledged. "Why do you think we should give you this post?"

Rishav waited for a few seconds to answer that, "Ma'am, I feel that I..."

"You feel?" the Eco person intervened.

"Uh, sorry, I *know* that I am the best person for this job. My man management skills and my leadership abilities will back me to complete any task given," he answered her query.

"Will you find time?" Kalsi followed.

"Definitely ma'am. I always have managed to do so."

"Do you have any girlfriend?" Veenu asked.

Rishav tittered on hearing this, "Ma'am?"

"You heard me right, go on. Tell us." Veenu added.

"No ma'am. I don't have a girlfriend," Rishav thought of Sahana almost instantly.

"How is it relevant Veenu?" Kalsi cut Ms. Sharma when she

was preparing herself for another go at Rishav.

Now why is she doing this to me? Rishav thought. Veenu Sharma knew Rishav well enough to not be asking these questions.

"How would you see your juniors?" The Physics teacher decided to pop in now.

Rishav was frustrated as none of his reforms were being asked about, *from girlfriend to juniors...what next? The name of my unborn child?*

"Sir, I will try and inspire a new group of leaders rather than create a new set of followers," Rishav said.

The guy who was the next closest thing to Chulbul Pandey of Dabangg fame, didn't get head to tail of what Rishav just said and instead muttered something that sounded like E=MC^2.

"Do you like fast food?" Veenu asked.

Kalsi on hearing this didn't even gather the energy to butt in. She dropped her pen and placed her hand on her forehead and looked at Veenu skeptically.

"Junk food? Yes ma'am definitely!" Rishav kind of had started liking the direction in which the interview was going. No serious questions, just a whole lot of crap. So much for wanting to be Head Boy, he atleast got to know what *really* happens in these so called *high profile* interviews.

"Your parents scold you for eating junk?" a follow up question. This time from Neeti Chopra whose gloominess had disappeared after supposedly being infected by the Veenu Virus.

"Yes ma'am they do."

"You fight with them?" Veenu asked.

Rishav's head swiftly turned to answer the question, "Yes ma'am at times."

"Haaaw, naughty boy!" her tone wasn't the best.

Kalsi sat there, with her palm covering her face. The expression of hers was hardly noticeable but it wouldn't really take knowledge of rocket-science to know how irritated she was seeing the discussion go awry.

Rishav looked out for another question. Maybe one asking whether his motions were clear or not, but nothing as such came. Kalsi could finally breathe a sigh of relief.

"If your questions are done..." she hissed. "...may I ask Rishav a final question?"

Everyone nodded in unison.

Kalsi kept an eye on Veenu all the while she spoke her sentence, "If not Head Boy, then what post shall you want to have?"

Rishav straightened his expressions; he was absolutely ready with his reply. With confidence oozing out of his voice, "Ma'am, I believe that if I ask for anything less than what I deserve then I deserve even less."

This time around a genuine smile reflected on Bindu's face. She took the comment in very good light it seemed, "All the best!" she said.

Sahana sat next to the balcony door, lost in the world of her thoughts.

She thought how she could escape the hell-hole of her life. She travelled through all the possibilities, thinking of all the places she could run away to. She just wanted to be alone.

She smiled sarcastically at the irony of the fact that she was alone in that house yet not alone enough to cry. She feared that it would warrant unnecessary attention to her. And the last thing she needed was her uncle to blame her for distracting her cousin again!

Sasha was a good person, so knew Sahana. She was bright enough just that at times Sasha lacked the determination. She took things too lightly. *Anyway*, Sahana thought. *I need to just stay here for a few months more and that's it!*

She tried to not think about what she had done a few days ago. It was so because if she looked at the angry red marks on her thigh, she would be tempted to do it again. When she was angry or upset, she just wanted the pain to go away. Hurting herself was one way to turn the mental pain into physical pain. The physical pain, according to her was easier to handle.

She often thought about why she lived at all. She was good for nothing. She wasn't good at dance, music, majorly sucked at public speaking and was just fine in studies. With what her uncle told her about the world out there, she would never get a job which could earn her her meals.

She took in a deep breath. She wondered, who'd remember her after she died. Who would care enough to remember her after her funeral? - None other than her parents, so she thought.

She rested her head against the door. She was sick and tired of everything surrounding her life. She wanted to start afresh. And college was the one place, where one could be a whole new person. But again, that was a good two years away. She longed to be nice to all; she wanted everyone to be happy; because she couldn't be happy if somebody else was unhappy. No matter how farfetched it sounded, but that was the way it was for Sahana. She put others happiness first.

Anyway, get over with the brooding bit, she forced herself to feel this way. ...*if you think anymore, you'll probably end up doing something that you'd regret and the scars wouldn't fade away for long.*

She got up, took her mobile, plugged in the earphones and switched on the radio with full volume. She grabbed her books and started studying.

A lot of times Sahana thought. A lot. But thinking according to her was not good. So she slept to not think, read books to not think, watched TV to not think.

But always, there was one second of the day when she thought of not living. She refused to like anyone. Boys spelled trouble and she could not at any cost, afford more trouble.

She thought of *him.* However, a little pretentious & blowing his own trumpet like he was, he was genuinely a nice person. At times, the thought of him as something more came to her mind. But she quickly dismissed it. She convinced herself not to like anyone and that meant *anyone.* A few people in the world were genuinely nice and according to her, he was one of them.

But they would just remain friends right? No need to get into all this relationship crap – boyfriend and girlfriend complexities!

She knew that he was trying to talk to her. It satisfied her vanity. She could see everything that he was thinking, read everything on his face. She could sense when he was trying to lead the conversation to past relationships. She could sense his desperate yet failed attempts to fix a meeting outside school (which he did, largely due to coincidence).

She didn't want all that and she was going to make sure he knew that pretty soon. He deserved the right to know, what all she thought about these sappy and crappy relationships.

SIXTEEN

Sahana walked towards her tuitions with much anticipation. It was the time she got away from that house where she lived. A house. Not a home.

She climbed up the stairs and saw that the peon was reading the newspaper with his legs up on the desk. Sahana raised an eyebrow. She wondered at the incongruity of his posture in the environment where the English teacher had particularly ordered them to maintain discipline.

"Aaj Sir *kahan hai bhaiyya*?" asked Sahana.

"Tuition cancelled *hai*," he replied without looking up from the paper.

Sahana hurried down the steps. For the first time in so many months, the teacher had cancelled a class. She was really happy about not studying for once.

She took out her phone and stared at the screen for long.

Whom should I call? She thought. *Vanya can't come. Nobody else would bother to come for an hour and then go back.*

Rishav would, of course!

Would he?

She dialed the number nonetheless. She would ask him where he was. If he was at his home and free only then will she tell him to come.

She waited for him to pick up. One ring…two…three…four.

"Dammit. Pick up, you ass," she said.

The number you have dialed is not answering this moment. Please try again later, the sing song voice said.

"Great. Nowhere to go," she said to herself.

She started walking towards her home when her phone vibrated. It was Rishav's number.

"Why didn't you pick up when I called you?" Sahana asked in an offensive voice.

"Because I didn't want you to waste your money. Mine is postpaid, you see," Rishav replied jokingly.

"Whatever. So tell me. Are you free *vaise*?" Sahana said choosing her words carefully.

"Yes. Why?" Rishav asked, excited that they were going to talk on the phone.

"Umm… My tuition's cancelled and I didn't want to go home. So I called you," Sahana replied with a little hesitation.

"Oh cool. So we can talk." Rishav said, while sitting upright on his bed.

"Actually, umm… I was thinking that you could umm… come here. Like you know it's not that far. My tuitions I mean, from my home. So it couldn't be far from your home, you know," Sahana said.

"Oh. Umm" Rishav jumped up from his bed as he tried to look for something good to wear in his wardrobe.

"If you don't want to come it's okay... Like really..." Sahana said sensing his hesitation.

"Oh no no... I want to come. Just tell me where exactly your tuition is," Rishav replied hurriedly.

Sahana gave him the directions of her tuitions.

"See you in ten then." Sahana said, with a hint of excitement in her voice.

"Yeah. Ten. Bye," Rishav replied while trying to not show too much of enthusiasm.

Sahana sat on a bench in a very tiny park. The grass was overgrown and yellow. She sat with her legs folded on the bench afraid that some insect or lizards might be crawling in that thick jungle of grass.

She played SNAKE on her mobile for 15 minutes until a voice interrupted her game.

"Hi." Rishav said while panting.

"Wait. I am about to beat Sasha's high score," Sahana said without caring to reply to his greeting.

Rishav looked at Sahana with astonishment.

"Umm... That's rude, you know" Rishav replied with a tone of disappointment.

"Uhuh," Sahana replied without looking at him.

"Donee," Sahana said with an enthusiastic tone.

"You're rude," Rishav replied.

"Yeah yeah, I know. I had to beat her score, you know. Plus you were panting. You needed time to breathe easily."

"True. But still...That's not how you greet your friends whom you've called from so far to meet you," Rishav said.

"Oh God. Will you get over it? And it's my choice how I greet people. If they don't like it, guess what? I couldn't care less about 'em. And you've come from near my sector and that's hardly 'so far', okay?"Sahana said with indignation."

"Fine, fine. Got over it," Rishav said, afraid that he would offend her and this chance of meeting her would go to waste if she got angry.

"Good. So what do you wanna do?"Sahana asked him while sitting on the bench with folded legs.

"Umm... talk?" Rishav replied as he sat next to her on the bench.

"No. That's stupid. If I wanted to talk I would've spoken to you on the phone, you dumbass," Sahana said.

"Oh yeah. Why are you sitting like this?" Rishav asked her.

"Because, idiot, the grass is not cut and there might be some insects lurking. Or snakes maybe? What if they crawl up my legs and bite me?"Sahana shuddered.

Rishav laughed uproariously.

"What's so funny? One could die you know," she said, offended.

"Oh God. Get up. Let's go eat *phuchkas*. Now don't ask me what *phuchkas* are," he said as he caught her hand and pulled her up.

"I know, ok? They are *gol gappes*" She replied.

"How did you know?" Rishav asked surprised that she knew the Bengali term for *gol gappes*.

"Long story."

"And we've got all the time in the world. Tell me all," he said.

She told the story about how she was watching this show where this Bengali girl was interviewed and she said that she loved *phuchkas* and a video was shown of her eating them.

"Wow. Even stupid TV shows can be quite informative at times," Rishav replied with a smile.

"Shut up, ok? There was nothing else on TV that day," Sahana replied.

They walked towards the street vendor and stood with their plates in their hands.

"I love 'em. Like really. In my hometown every corner has them."

"No wonder you're so into eating," Rishav taunted.

"Oh please, ok? I eat because I am depressed," Sahana said while popping the huge *gol gappa* in her mouth.

"And why are you depressed?" Rishav asked, intrigued that someone like her was suffering from depression.

"It's a depressing story. And I don't want to talk about it. It is family stuff," Sahana said, while she wiped the water she spilled on her shirt.

"It's good to share. The burden lessens you know? Why don't you talk to Vanya about it?" Rishav said.

"Wow. I haven't thought of that before," she said with sarcasm dripping from her voice, "Oh my god. You are so intelligent. How can I ever thank you?".

"I was just giving some advice," Rishav shrugged.

"I think I have enough people in my life giving me unwanted advice. I definitely don't need another one."

"Okay, okay. No advice. Fine?" Rishav said, raising his hand in the air.

"Yeah," she murmured.

"*Waise* if you want to share something, I am all ears. I won't tell anyone anything. Promise," Rishav said in a meaningful tone.

"I know you won't tell anybody. But it's boring... and depressing... and sad. And uhhh...what's worse than that?"She asked.

Rishav paid the vendor and they walked towards the park. Sahana sat with her legs folded.

"They are not gonna eat you," Rishav said.

"Yes, yes. The omniscient Rishav Sen knows that the poisonous insect living in this jungle will not bite me. Right?"

"Oh god. *Ab* tell me already?" he pleaded.

"What?" Sahana asked.

"Umm your sad story?" Rishav asked.

"Oh that. Well you see..." Sahana began telling him the story of her life.

After an hour, Sahana looked at her mobile and shouted. "Oh crap. I am late."

"It's okay. Take an auto," Rishav said, trying to calm Sahana down.

"God! What am I gonna do?" Sahana panicked.

"It's okay *bubah*. We'll grab an auto. It'll take max five minutes," Rishav said.

"Let's go," Sahana grabbed his hand and they ran towards an auto on the main road.

Rishav didn't ask for the fare. It didn't matter. She had to get home. It was already dark. And from what he had heard of her life, he was pretty scared.

"What the fuck will I say to them?" Sahana asked herself as she bit her nails.

"*Bhaiyya, jaldi*" Rishav told the auto driver. "It's fine. You'll reach. Say that the rickshaw was charging you too much and you had to walk. Ok?" Rishav explained to Sahana, trying to calm her down.

"Yeah okay. Fine. Urggggghh...my life," Sahana groaned.

"Listen, Sahana. You'll get out of this murk soon enough. You need to keep your head till then. Okay? Don't do anything stupid. Geddit?" Rishav said.

"Yeah," Sahana said with a sad smile.

She looked up at Rishav and said, "Don't tell anyone. Okay? Not even your best friend, your mom or your dad. No one. This will go to your grave. If I find out that you did, you are so dead." Sahana said with an assertive tone.

"Yeah yeah, Like you can. *Ab chal. Tera sector aagaya hai,"* Rishav replied while laughing.

Sahana hit him.

"Shut up," she said.

She got out of the auto before her sector's gate. The sky was already dark and the street was deserted.

"Thanks for coming," Sahana said to Rishav as he got out of the auto too.

"The pleasure was entirely mine, miss," Rishav said with a bow.

"Right," she said. She leaned and gave him a kiss on the cheek.

"Bye" she said as she ran like a penguin towards her sector's gate as Rishav's ears went from pink to red in the speeding auto.

SEVENTEEN

Sahana could point out all the flaws in men (the worst half of species, she felt). All of them really! She could make fun of their perversion, their desperation, their pathetic behavior and their freakiness. The last thing that Sahana wanted was to get cozy with one of the freaks as she called them. She looked at couples and felt nauseas instantly. All that sappy and so called conventional stuff didn't work for her.

Sometimes, she did think about the perfect guy for her but in her immediate veinity, she couldn't find a guy who even remotely resembled him (not Rishav, her dream man rather).

She was going towards the Accounts section of the school alone when Rishav stopped her in her tracks. "Where are you going?"

"Well, how does it matter to you?" she replied.

"Well it doesn't matter much …just that if you want some company, I am happy to oblige."

Poor guy, she thought. *I shouldn't make him try so hard.*

She shrugged and he followed.

They were walking in silence when Sahana noticed some juniors ahead. She saw a couple with their hands loosely tangled in each other's and she couldn't help but gawk. She pointed it out to Rishav. "See that, that's what I don't like – holding hands! So cheesy!"

Rishav didn't reply. All that he could think was that this girl was way too complicated and one hell of a piece of work. Whether he had the energy to untangle the big mess Sahana was, was the big question.

On the other hand, Sahana wished that he'd understand she was not playing hard to get but just that she wanted him to stop trying to want more.

After a few more moments of silence and a few steps ahead, Rishav spoke, "Maybe they like it. Maybe that's the way to show their love for each other."

"True. But I am saying that *I* don't like it. Not that *they* don't like it."

"Okay," he mumbled a faint reply.

"Relationships..." continued Sahana. "...are useless, meaningless and a big waste of time! I don't like them because in the end, I know that one day or the other, those two are gonna break up and I don't think I have time or the energy to cope with all of that. Plus, I don't like relationships because you would have to tell your boyfriend or girlfriend everything about yourself which could be turned against you, if you happen to break up. Hence, the conclusion is that they are *hazardous*."

"You don't have to tell anyone anything. You can omit some things, sometimes," Rishav replied to her long statement.

"That's the thing *na*. See, if I have a boyfriend, then he would expect me to talk to him on the phone. But I can't do that because of certain restrictions and stuff. And when I tell him that, he would want to know more…how and why? And I can't tell him, because in the event of a fall out, he might just tell It to his friends. And I can't let that happen, can I?" she finally ended.

"True," he said.

"Do you know any other word that that?" she asked.

"Anyway," Sahana continued without waiting for a reply. "I sincerely hope that you don't feel too highly of relationships, or else we might have problems getting along!" she sounded blunt.

"Why, of course…" said Rishav as he made his way across the winding corridors of Delhi High School.

Bindu Kalsi stared into the sheet that she was carrying with her on stage. She had scribbled a few key-notes on what to say and on what not to say on stage. But much to her annoyance, she left that sheet back within the comforts of her cabin. She strained her eyes to scan through the list of names.

She looked up and let out a deep breath of air. She paused and observed the students standing, all so silent, waiting in baited breath to hear something they had been anticipating for over a month now. Almost everything in DHS had revolved around the Council appointments, hence, every single child, teacher and parent alike knew its importance. With the growing silence, grew impatience. Many thought of it to be a dramatic prologue to what Bindu would say but few knew that Bindu was utilizing that time to make up stuff she would have to say. She was bad with speeches.

"Good morning…" she said in a nasal tone.

"Gooood morniiiing ma'am…!" There was a stretched out, enthusiastic reply from the juniors while the seniors standing near the back found it below their levels of coolness to actually wish the Principal back.

"As you already know that we have assembled here for a specific purpose. And that is to introduce you all to your new set of leaders," she paused briefly to see how people were responding. As expected, everyone pretty much had blank expressions.

"We had some really good interviews over the past week or so and we have taken a lot of pain to select the *best* council possible!" she added. "So, these badge bearers will be our representatives in the student community. Respect them and seek help from them whenever required. If they break rules, report them but at no time will you misbehave with them. Is that understood?"

"Yessss maaaaam!" another sing-song reply.

"Good," she said. "I will read out the names, one by one. Starting from the Head Boy and Head Girl and follow it up with the Vice Head Boy and so on."

Two people from within those three thousand were barely managing to breathe.

Jai tried hard appearing cool. It seemed that his calmness had just gone on a vacation. He constantly scratched his head, shifted weight from one leg to the other and rubbed his stubble unnecessarily. He snapped at people who were muttering things like, 'congrats' and 'you'll be the Head Boy', around him. He desperately needed some peace of mind; the last few nights had been terrible for him, to say the least. Sleepless nights and then when he finally managed to get some sleep, he was haunted by nightmares of Rishav Sen running around in his father's dressing gown. It was three years back that Jai was identified as a possible candidate to become the Head Boy and ever since, he had succeeded without any competition. He did whatever he could within his control and also stuff beyond his control to ensure that the moment he was facing went according to plan. *Nothing can ruin it,* he thought. He'd probably start crying if the results turned out to be unfavourable – such was his desperation for that post.

On the other hand, in a more contrasting scenario – Rishav Sen stood chatting and cracking a few jokes with people around him. All of a sudden it seemed that these posts didn't matter to him, he was a different person altogether. *I've got nothing to lose,* he told himself, the moment negative thoughts started creeping in.

Sahana glanced at Rishav from a little far away, she was afraid that he might just go all emotional if he didn't get the post. She interrupted Vanya a number of times, just to stand on her toes and keep a check on how Rishav was responding. She was anxious too but she wasn't too sure on why her heart prayed that Rishav *didn't* get the post.

Siddhant Dalvi, stuck to his usual self. He wasn't even considered for interview. His chances were all gone and he muttered a chant under his breath that wished Rishav, good luck with his application.

The attention shifted back to the stage. "And the names are…" said Bindu Kalsi.

"…for Head Boy, we have," she began her sentence. "…for Head Boy, it is Jai Chauhan!" she said.

And the response was incomparable to anything that had ever happened in school before. A sea of thunderous claps engulfed the entire school as there was hooting, screaming and cheering for one of the most popular heroes and figures that stood by the 'cool' image of Delhi High School. Students of all shapes and sizes, teachers and assistant teachers alike – all clapped for Jai as hard as they could. Jai got all pumped up and screamed out a few abuses in the air as he walked briskly towards the stage, bisecting the crowd, occasionally pushing them to make way for himself. And when he was almost through the crowd and nearly reaching the stair case of the stage and when the noise and euphoria had died down, Bindu Kalsi spoke again. "And by discretion as the Principal of DHS, we will be having a slight change in the system," she said in one go.

Jai stopped in his tracks; he looked at the Principal with a startled expression. *Bhenchod, what the fuck is she saying?* He thought.

As an answer to all the curious faces looking up at her, Bindu Kalsi clarified. "Using my discretion, I announce that this year in lieu of a Vice Head Boy – we shall be having *two* Head Boys!" she laid enough emphasis on words she had to.

Some kind of bomb seemed to have exploded because right then, the chatter got replaced by a buzz that spread like wildfire. There were a string of whispers that ran through all present there. Teachers looked at each other with surprised expressions, students pro-Jai cursed Kalsi while the neutral ones tried hard to come to terms with what was announced.

What's wrong with this fuckin' woman!" scowled Jai. He nonetheless, grumpily, walked ahead and got onto the stage.

"As the second Head Boy, we have an equally deserving candidate – someone who in a short while has done wonders for the school and I am sure he will not let me down. The second Head Boy of DHS, please come up on stage, Rishav Sen!" she announced with great pride. She smiled like never before.

The moment he heard his name, Rishav's heart burst into an array of emotions. He couldn't think and feel like a normal human being then. All he wanted had just come true and it would take something more than time to help him come to terms with it. His vision was blurry, there were people patting him, some shook his hands. He could feel people grabbing him and congratulating in their own personal way but Rishav tried hard searching for the face he wanted to see the most. He looked all around frantically to locate her. He needed to catch a glimpse of her before he went on to the stage and there she was.

He finally managed to see Sahana, a little away from where he stood. She was visible, yet concealed from his view in a way.

She was smiling. They looked at each other for a few seconds, Rishav smiled back. Some kind of unspoken communication took place between them. He wanted to thank her for being there in his life and give her a hug to let her know how special she was, but then came the second call for him. With a quick last look, Rishav broke into a jog and tried reaching the stage before his dream ended…

EIGHTEEN

Rishav stood on stage with the twenty other students who were privileged enough to be chosen for the Council. And the list did include the likes of Hardik, Chintan, Tarun and Rishi. In short, most of Jai's ass lickers had found their way into the Council – much to the delight of Jai.

If one felt that Rishav's tough times had ended, well then it wasn't to be – as the tough times had just begun for him.

The moment Rishav's name was announced, there was an immediate lull that crept in. Everyone had an opinion, but no one was sure enough to share that opinion. As a result of that, Rishav didn't get the most overwhelming response like Jai did. His was a more lukewarm one.

He could hear a few boos too, mostly coming from the senior lot. There were some derogatory remarks too, as he moved through the crowd. And finally when he reached the stage, Jai's expression was that of a person whose pride had been hurt. And when you puncture the ego of the royalty, you don't really escape unscathed.

Rishav nervously glanced at Sahana, from above the stage. She seemed all confident and chirpy. He looked around, while the Principal spoke. He saw the faces and apart from a couple of guys – Rishav couldn't really relate to a single person. Yet, he was there – the Head Boy of Delhi High School.

The road that lay ahead was a difficult one as he would have to slog his butt out to manage to hold on to this post. By the end of Class XI, only one student would be retained as Head Boy and the other would be relegated to a lower post. And this decision would be taken purely on a merit basis – so said the almanac. However, Rishav knew how heavy Veer Chauhan's wallet was and how good Jai's chances were of retaining the post.

A lot of tact was required and for an impulsive, passionate fool like Rishav Sen; tact was something difficult to achieve.

You did it! Congrats," said Sahana, all smiling.

"Yes, I did," Rishav replied, slightly morose over the response he had just got.

"What happened? You should be happy, Mr. Head Boy." She tried her best to cheer him up.

"Happy over the fact that they booed me? Yes, right! I am happy, see..." he grinned artificially.

"God. Are you kidding me? You are sad because those ugly superficial bastards didn't cheer?" she replied.

"Uh huh," he started moving towards the school building. Sahana closely followed.

" Would you get over it already? Where's my treat first? Gimme my treat and then you can depressed as much as you want" she asked.

"Yeah, sure. Let's celebrate that a loser just became the Head

Boy!" he exclaimed.

"It doesn't matter. And I think a person who is sensible and who has enough brains to comprehend logic would get that," Sahana said as she grabbed his arm to ensure that Rishav got every word of what she was saying.

He remained silent, she continued, "They either want you to be cool in lingo and behavior and stuff or hot by appearance. And since, you are none – they kind of don't accept you as much as they accept Jai. No offence intended," she smiled slyly as she explained it to him.

"That's really flattering, Sahana. And what do you mean by - I am not accepted? Are you trying to make me feel better or worse?" he sounded pissed.

"Why do you take so much of offense for no reason? Just listen will you?" she insisted.

"No, thank you!" he fastened his steps. She walked quicker to catch up with him.

"Sen, you are annoying me now. Don't show me your anger, geddit?"

"Um, excuse me," he stopped midway. "But I'm not showing you my frustration. I am just telling you that my sadness is kind of justified.

"To a certain extent, yes. But just because some people don't clap for you doesn't make you a loser. They are not as familiar with you as they are with Jai. And I order you to be not sad when I am around. When I am not, well then you can scream, shout, mourn, or whatever you want to do." she said sweetly. He smiled. "Where's my hug?" he asked.

"You don't ask for a hug. Ok? It's weird."

"Oh shut up. Just tell me if I am getting it or not?"

"Horny bastard. Stay away," she said while taking her tongue out.

"And what if I say that a hug is the cure to my sadness?" A lopsided grin reappeared, "Go to Veenu, she'll give you a *tight* hug, I am sure," she laughed.

Rishav almost had a pretty disjointed sentence formed in his head when she started speaking again

"You get it when you earn it. Just like that chocolate, you know. That fine, dark delicious chocolate." she said the last bit while licking her lips.

"Hahaaa. Fine, fine…no hugs. Happy? But I get to treat you don't I?" they entered the classroom and took their window seats.

"Yes you do. Chinese, bitch. Mainland China. Nothing less than that will be accepted." she said in a dead serious tone. Rishav's jaw dropped for a moment, "What?" "Mainland China, isn't it like a little too…"

" *Tres* expensive? Yes, I know," she completed him. "But I still want you to treat me there." She took her tongue out.

"Alright," Rishav said hesitantly as his mind started working on how he would arrange for cash that would sustain a date at Mainland China.

Sahana broke into laughter as she saw Rishav's face contort. "I was just pulling your leg. Don't worry I won't burn a hole in your pockets like your girlfriends will do in the future. Get me Crackle if you want to. Ok? Money to me, *mon ami*, doesn't matter. Remember that."

And just when Rishav was going to say something really praiseworthy of Sahana, she put a few more words to her previous sentence.

"Though if you see it practically money does matter you know…" she said. "…or else, you know, I can't really kill all my options of being treated by you at expensive places," she winked.

Rishav rolled his eyes. "Will you give me the chance to drop you back home again today?"

"Again? Umm…Wasn't it like just a week back?" she asked.

"Didn't you eat food, like just yesterday?" he countered.

"So, you are comparing yourself to food?"

"Yes, I am a necessity in your life," he calmly replied.

"Nothing other than money is a necessity, babe. Stop flirting with me now." she gave hints of her snappy self.

"Oh yes, trying too hard am I now?" Rishav casually mentioned.

"Whoa! When did I say *that?*" she was surprised.

He knows that I think he tries too hard. Wow, she thought.

"Yeah, I said something about you feeling that I try too hard," he took off his glasses.

She narrowed her eyes, "I don't feel that at all. Stop assuming things. It's what they say when you assume, you make an ASS of U and ME." she stuttered. She tried looking in all directions but at Rishav.

"Okay. But you should know that I do know how you feel. It's not just you who gets to read what I think and understand what I am feeling," he added.

A semi-stunned Sahana looked on as he spoke. "…at times, even I get to know what's going on in your head. Remember that and now, I seriously need to go and use the washroom," saying so, Rishav said while patting her arm and walked past her towards the classroom door.

God. I so don't like him. Or do I?

"Head Boy!" Jai sneered, on seeing Rishav approach.

"Yes, Jai, I thought as much," Rishav replied. "I was merely going to congratulate you on getting what you wanted and you spoiled my mood."

"I didn't spoil anything *Bengali*, you are like a cone stuck up my ass, didn't want this day. Trust me."

Rishav nodded, "We can't really do anything can we? Guess, we have to work together."

"We don't *have* to work together Rishav Sen. I won't change my ways and I am very hard to share power with."

"I realized that already Jai. All that I am saying is that the school's interests lie before our personal egos. Appreciate the fact that you are accountable to the school and not the other way," Rishav tried hard.

Jai started laughing. He mimicked Rishav in an uncouth manner. "*Tu chutiya hai*," he said.

Rishav smiled, "Thank you!"

"Hahahaa..." laughed Jai as some of his ass-lickers came by to see the drama. "He's such a cunt, I just called him a *chutiya* and he says *thank you*."

The people around him started laughing too. Jai landed a heavy arm on Rishav's shoulder.

"Dude, bad times are in store for you. I was always going to be the Head Boy and even though there'd be two badges this time around – my badge would be the one with the real power with it, okay?" Jai pointed out.

"We shall see to that, don't take tension so easily. After all, you too will have to work with me for a year now. Who knows what happens at the end of the day!"

"Ha ha...I know what happens at the end of the day. Ever heard of Veer Chauhan, you *son of a bitch?*"

"Yes, I have Jai. Your respected dad and the owner of *Skytel*, I know of him."

"Then you should also know where he stands and where his son stands," he started scratching his head like an eight year old chimp.

"As far as I know, his son is standing right in front of me and is no more powerful than what Rishav Sen is in this school," Siddhant on seeing Rishav in a sticky situation, badly outnumbered, decided to stand up for his friend. And there he was, right next to Rishav, backing him up in this verbal duel.

There were calls of *aam-chutiya*, the moment Jai's friends saw Siddhant arrive.

"Oh, look who's here…*aaam-chuutiyyaaa!"* Jai's comments ended with a roar of laughter and some high fives from his friends.

"You know and so do I know Jai, what all you've done over the past few years to come to this place. If not others then just pity yourself for what you've become, you power hungry moron. And I am proud that Rishav Sen, Head Boy of Delhi High School is a friend of mine," Siddhant spoke with a lot of confidence for a change.

"One of," mumbled Jai who was more interested in catching Siddhant saying something wrong that he could turn against him at any given moment.

"I am proud because even without enough years spent in this school, without having Veer Chauhan as his father, without buying his way out of every tough situation in life, Rishav Sen would be standing right next to you when the oath would be taken. He will be sworn in as the Head Boy and you, your dad and his money can do *shit* about it. You can never be a Rishav, no matter how much you'd want to be one."

Jai did not respond, he chose to stay silent. Seeing him, so did his ass lickers.

"*Arre o Sambha, main toh senti ho gya re!*" Jai exclaimed. His remarks drew large rounds of laughter and sniggered comments from those around him.

"One *chutiya* joins forces with another *chutiya,*" Jai laughed. "Expect *Kaun Banega Chutiya* next, eh?"

Rishav and Siddhant couldn't come up with a reply quick enough. But someone else did.

Tired of over hearing constant jibes at someone who meant a lot to her and fed up with Jai's arrogance, Sahana couldn't take a word more.

She walked and stood in front of Jai with her hands tightly crossed in front of her.

"You son of a dog," she said in almost a whisper. "You are worse than the fungus that grows after a street dog pees on an electric pole. And don't you DARE COME NEAR THEM AGAIN. YOU FUCKING UNDERSTAND?"She screamed the last bit while pushing Jai violently.

Jai fell back and tripped on a stone and landed with a thump on the ground.

"He gets enough attention already," Sahana said to Rishav and Siddhant. "I don't think you need to feed that ego anymore. Bloody scum. Let's just get out of here okay?" she tugged Rishav as she walked away from that place.

Hardik whispered into Jai's ears, "*Tera toh katta ho gya!*"

Jai changed into a deeper tone of red. "Fuck you *bhenchods*!" he shouted and stormed off.

"I appreciate what you did for me but never ever do this okay?" Rishav curtly pointed out to a visibly angry Sahana.

"Do what? That asshole deserved a kick on the crotch. But then I would've had to dirty my shoes you know. Had I stood there for a second more, I would've done that too, you know." she said as though it was a matter of fact. But Rishav could sense how angry she was.

"Calm down Sahana, it doesn't matter."

"Maybe not to you, but for me, yes. My friend's insult is my insult. For once, quit being such a girl and go and confront him."

"Why should I? Isn't he miserable enough already? Can't you see the freakin' insecurity in his eyes? Ever since he's lost his mom – he remains insecure about everything that money can't buy. Sympathise with him Sahana," Rishav plead.

"My sympathies are not sold on the pavement; I have none for the likes of Jai and Co. who think that the world is under their feet because of fuckin' money in their pockets," Sahana had got hyper and that meant more swinging of arms and more neck movements.

"I see your point, but…"

"No, you don't see my point. If you did, you would have supported me rather than being such a loser about it," she said. She was pacing the floor of their empty classroom. It was a PT period and all but two of them had gone outside to sweat it out in the Sun.

"I do support you but tell me something, the truth will always remain the truth wouldn't it? Jai saying things about me that intend to hurt me would just be *opinions* and opinions in no way influence the truth," he said calmly.

"They do, you big dumbass! They make the reality appear differently. And that is exactly what you should challenge."

"Sahana, we clearly differ in our point of view, could we not talk about it? Please?" he asked.

"No, if you want it to happen then clearly we need to resolve these issues. I don't want to be seen around with a sissy. You can't stand up for yourself, how would you ever stand up for me?" she charged at him.

"Lower your voice..." Rishav hissed. "There are classes going on here and besides, I *am* the Head Boy right? Jai can do nothing about it, he knows that and everyone does. So why should I respond unnecessarily?"

Sahana didn't reply. She was still burning with rage. Some kind of silence transcended upon them and that silence sent both of them into realization mode and the much sought after realization did strike after all.

"Listen. I am really glad you did that for me. But Siddhant was already there. Why exactly did you do that?"Rishav asked her in a sweet whisper as he put his hand on her arm.

Sahana took his hand from her arm and placed it in her hand.

"Get up," she said.

"Why?" he asked as he got up. He could feel the goose bumps on his neck.

"Come here," she said as she hugged him tightly.

Rishav put his hands on her back and held tightly.

They stood like that for how long, Rishav didn't know. But he didn't want to let go.

"Now let me go, you idiot," Sahana said laughing.

Sahana kissed his neck and pulled out her arms. Rishav placed a kiss on her cheek. He could see that her face was completely red.

"Feel *le li*?"Sahana said, putting her tongue out.

"Oh yes," Rishav slyly smiled.

NINETEEN

"Sahana, I have been assigned duty today, won't be in class. Mind taking down the notes for me please?" Rishav asked while he dumped his bag on top of his desk in haste.

"What duty?" she asked.

She had washed her hair; it was left open. Rishav gawked at her for a few seconds. She wasn't conventionally the most beautiful around but wasn't someone who wouldn't catch your eye either. *She looks stunning*, he thought.

"Yeah yeah, stop gazing at my pretty face. I know I look good today," she teased. "What duty?" she asked again.

"Some French Exchange programme," he said. "I have to stand there beside A. Chandrashekhar, all the while he goes about with his long speech and then I also have to ensure that everyone's on duty and that no-one's making out in the green room."

He smirked when he said *making out*. Sahana looked at him with a wry smile, "I have a cold today."

"So?" Rishav asked. "Why are you telling me this?"

"Just like that," she replied. "I just wanted you to know."

"Hmm…so will you or will you not?" he pinned his badge that read *Head Boy* next to his name.

"Of course not!" Sahana hissed.

"You won't take down notes for me?" he re-checked.

"Notes? Huh?" she was thinking of something else. It was pretty evident to Rishav from the way she replied but he chose to act dumb for the time being. "Notes? Yeah of course, I shall take down your notes!" she fumbled while she spoke.

"Then what was the no for?" he asked.

"Umm…nevermind! So? You have to go right?"

"Yeah, in about five minutes," he said hesitantly.

"Cool. Why five minutes? Go now," she replied.

"You have a problem if I wait for five minutes?"

"Umm…for what exactly?"

"I dunno. Just like that, talk to you maybe?" Rishav shrugged.

"I see, couldn't you realize that before you took up your goddamn duty? Huh?" she sounded pissed.

"Sahana, it's *my duty*, I can't run away from it. I need to prove that I am better that Jai."

"Yes, that's all you care about- proving to the world that you aren't a loser. Eh?"

"Oh God! Here you go again…Sahana try to understand my perspective." He tried convincing her, but in vain.

"Nopes, there's no need. It's okay Rishav. Your five minutes are up really and if you don't mind I need to put my head down and sleep, so bye!" she rested her head on the desk. She looked in the other direction.

"Sahana? Angry?" he gently caressed her hair.

"No, just go now okay?" she pushed his hand away.

"I'll miss you, see you later," he said as he retracted and turned around to leave.

She didn't reply. *Women,* Rishav thought.

"Hello Muskaan, how do you do?" the Chairman guffawed without any reason.

"I am good Sir, how are you?" she bent her knees slightly to greet him.

"Sit, sit," said Kalsi, popping a biscuit in her mouth.

"And you called for me? For?" Muskaan inquired.

"Wanted to know about Socialact Wave, I've heard that we've got sponsorships double the amount this year?" the Chairman asked.

"Indeed sir. We have. And thanks to the ever patronizing Veer Chauhan, he nearly paid up seventy percent of the total amount," she took great care to ensure that every word that left her mouth was politically correct.

"Old Veer eh?" the Chairman chuckled. "Came to me once searching for a job, his IIT degree was taking him nowhere. I got him associated with this Heeru Balwani guy. Now look where Veer is," there was a hint of arrogance in A.Chandrashekhar's voice.

Both Kalsi and Muskaan nodded upon hearing what he had to say.

"So, Veer's son...what's his name again, erm?" he tried recollecting the name.

"...Jai!" He said. "Yes, so is Jai being well looked after?"

"Yes he is. He is one of our Head Boys this year," that often missing smile was now Bindu Kalsi's face.

"Head Boy, that's great news. But two? Why Bindu?" he asked her directly.

"It's partly my decision Sir," Muskaan intervened.

"Your decision? How? You weren't even in the Selection Committee," he said.

"But you do know how things are when it comes to me," Muskaan looked into the eyes of the Chairman.

"Yes, but what's the idea behind this then?"

"You see…" Kalsi began, only to be interrupted by Muskaan.

"It is about how we want our school to be seen to the outside world," said Muskaan. "Jai is a symbol of the aristocracy in our school; he represents the rich and the influential. DHS is proud to have the elite of the society within its walls. On the other hand, Rishav Sen is the symbol of hard work and determination. He's a dedicated young idealist who wants to change the world; he has made a name for himself despite not having an equivalent backup system like that of Jai. And that's what makes these two contrasting people so interesting. Their cases will be a talking point in years to come and this decision was a part of the agenda to make DHS a more viable brand."

A.Chandrashekhar changed his posture slightly and carried on to listen with intent.

Muskaan paused briefly and continued, "Representatives of two different sides makes the scenario far more interesting than what it already is. The meritorious will see Rishav to be a symbol of hope, someone who can stand out despite all the odds. While, the rich and powerful will see what a little bit of support did to Jai and the same could happen with their sons and daughters too. You see, this makes the parents want to die to put their children into Delhi High School. All this hoopla and hype, it benefits us immensely. Increase the fees, demand donations, do whatever you want to – the brand goes on. And by ensuring that both sides are equally happy, we have actually taken the first step towards ensuring that we meet a long term goal – *dominance*."

"You mean to say, all of this was discussed before you all selected the Head Boy, boys in this case?" he asked.

"This information was restricted to just Muskaan and I. And now that you know, I hope that you do realize that it's in the best interests of the school that it doesn't go out," Bindu Kalsi sounded guarded in the way she spoke. "This was an idea of sheer brilliance, wasn't it Sir?"

"Yes indeed. It was a great idea," the Chairman exclaimed. "Muskaan, sharp mind you've got here. Eh?"

Muskaan Kaur took a superficial bow which was far from displaying humility.

After a few moments of silence, the Chairman spoke again. "What do you say Bindu, we need a Vice Principal for DHS International, what about Muskaan?" he looked at Kalsi while he spoke.

Kalsi let the sentence register before she replied, "Why not? I think it is a *great* idea!"

Muskaan grinned, "It's going to be an honour, truly grateful!"

"But…?" said Kalsi.

"But what?" the Chairman asked.

"Wouldn't it be an issue that Muskaan has held absolutely no position of administrative authority till now? How will you convince the board?" Kalsi seemed concerned.

"Hmmm…." The chairman went into deep thought. "Unless, we provide her with some experience, for the sake of showing it on her bio-data. What say?"

"That is an interesting idea. I have been wanting to replace Veenu for a long time now, her jokes and self-applauses have become annoying now," Kalsi said with a sigh.

"We cannot replace Veenu, she is the safest, most gullible and clean people around. She does no harm to others, we won't get much by replacing her," Muskaan butted in.

"She is right," A.Chandrashekhar said out loud. "Don't we have Madhuri's position empty?"

"Yes, we do. So should we put her there?" Kalsi asked.

"Yes, yes, go ahead. It's an internal decision and we'll call it a stop-gap arrangement so that it is away from probing eyes. Once the session is over, we can immediately shift Muskaan to DHS International as its Vice Principal. What do you think?"

"Brilliant idea!" said Kalsi.

"And I second her," said Muskaan.

The Chairman took out his cell phone and dialed a number. "I am going to send you an email from my mobile, within ten minutes. Forward it to all members of the board, get me?" he waited for the person's reply before hanging up.

TWENTY

Siddhant was unsure about what he had just done. Taking on one of the most influential faces in the school wasn't the best thing to do. But he did what he felt was right and that was something that kept him content.

He crossed the road in front of DHS, took a right and started walking towards his house that was a few hundred meters away. The stress of approaching exams, constant jibes from his peers and added workload had made his life terrible. Add to that, the annoying heat – life was difficult.

As he made his way, barely a few yards away from his house, a car stopped by. The window panes rolled down, Chintan flashed a wry smile. "*Abbe o kutte*," he shouted out.

"Motherfucker, do you even know what you say these days? And to whom?"

Siddhant ignored and started walking again.

The car caught up with him again, in no time.

"Running away loser?" Chintan asked.

Chintan threw an empty Diet Coke can at him. "Next time motherfucker, it'll be something harder. Beware." The window panes rolled up again and the car sped past.

Siddhant turned around to spot a few juniors cracking jokes on him. They stopped immediately on seeing him. He shook his head in disgust and chose to ignore them.

On reaching home, he flung his bag across the dining room and stormed into his room. He shut the door behind him and punched the wall hard. *Why me?* He asked in frustration.

In the meanwhile, his mom knocked on the door, "Lunch *beta*?" she asked.

"Not now!" he replied.

"What happened?" she knocked again.

He didn't reply.

"Reply *beta*, anything in school? You didn't complete your assignments? Teachers scolded you *kya*?" she asked unknowing of how complex life in schools had become. It was no longer about just not completing your assignments on time.

"Leave me alone!" he said in a croaky tone.

She got a little paranoid, "Open the door!"

"I said not *now!* Why don't you understand?"

"Have your lunch, it will get cold, I will help you complete your assignment today," his mom said, still quite presumptuous.

"For the last time…" said Siddhant as he removed the latch of his door. He faced his mom, "…it is *not* about stupid assignments!" he shouted out.

"Why are you shouting?" she asked. "Lunch?" she held the plate right under his nose.

He lost all control of himself and in a momentary fit of rage; he took hold of the plate and flung it across the room. The food spilled all over the place and the plate landed quite near the TV. His mother retracted and looked in horror at what had just become of her son.

"Siddhant!" she shouted out. "What's wrong with you?"

"Nothing…can't you understand? Just *leave me alone!*" tears started rolling down his cheeks. He controlled them with a lot of difficulty.

"I WANT TO BE ALONE!" he screamed at her. "Get lost mom!"

"But Siddhant?" she was about to reply. But, he turned around and shut the door on her face. He dug his head inside his pillow and started crying about what had become of him.

All these years, he had spent trying to gain acceptance – but what he managed was the tag of a pushover. The *aam-chutiya* as people called him. For once, he stood up for a friend. Took on a character, he had detested for a long period of time and he is chucked cans at in front of his juniors. He is abused publically. He is humiliated, day in and day out.

It was because he couldn't speak the cool lingo, he couldn't play a guitar or have nice pick up lines for chicks. He was a loser because despite all the certificates he had, he wasn't even considered for a single competition, a single respectable post in the Council. His dreams meant nothing to the world and so was the same for him.

He walked up to his drawer and opened it. He took out the pile of certificates that his parents had meticulously collected over the years. He scanned through them. They dated back to as old as his Montessori Merit Cards. He tore them all, he chucked the medals into the dustbin and tore every certificate that he could find. He broke the plastic trophies that he had got, things that were of no value to the world. Once he was done, he repeatedly hit his head on the wall and kept on cursing himself.

His mother who was by now in a state of shock was silently sobbing away in the adjacent room. Siddhant's quest for acceptance had ended even before it had begun.

"Muskaan will be taking over as the Vice Principal, soon," Rishav said as Sahana and he, waited for the next train to arrive.

"What?"

"I said that Muskaan will be taking over as the Vice Principal, soon!" Rishav reiterated.

"Of course I heard that! Why did you repeat?" Sahana snapped.

"You just said *what?* That's why I repeated!"

"Don't you understand? My '*what*' was like *what the fuck?* More of an exclamatory statement than a question," she replied.

"Okay okay, I get it! Can we *not* discuss the different connotations of the word *what*?"

"Yeah, whatever!" she answered back.

"So, as I was saying, erm...yeah, Muskaan! Such a bitch she is *yaar!* She finally became the VP!" Rishav said. There was a loud horn, the next Metro had arrived. The waiting passengers suddenly came back to life upon hearing the loud noise. They started approaching the edge of the platform in anticipation of the train to come to a halt. Impatience and lack of knowledge of the sentence – *after you,* the Delhi public could be really annoying when it came to travelling with.

Bulky men pushed and shoved whoever came by their way. The frail looking Rishav Sen thought it to be his moral responsibility to be ensuring that no harm came Sahana's way. He tried using his 'utterly masculine' arms to prevent anyone from randomly hitting Sahana. And his kind gesture was rewarded with a curt comment, "What on earth are you trying to do? Keep your hands to yourself – they are kind of girly; and I can take care of myself!"

He opened his mouth to argue but then realized how futile that would be and hence, decided to keep quiet.

They entered the train and failed to get a seat. Sahana made a face.

"So…" she said. "…what about your mom then? Did she tell you the news? Is she happy about all of this?"

"My mom? You mean my self-proclaimed mom? Veenu Ma'am?" Rishav confirmed.

Sahana nodded.

"…Oh, she *toh* is perfectly fine. These petty things hardly matters to her. I pity the others who've been eyeing Madhuri's post with a lot of interest. You know, that Physics guy, the megalomaniac – what's his name again?"

"Suraj Singh," Sahana replied.

"Oh yes! Suraj Singh, he was quite interested in Madhuri's post from Day One. Poor guy that he would have to be content with playing action-reaction with his Physics apparatus!"

"Speaking of Suraj Singh," she began. "…you know he's such a jerk, he scratches his crotch in front of his students."

Rishav raised an eyebrow, "I definitely, do *not* want to go on that track." He chuckled.

Both of them fell silent for a while till she broke it, "So, Muskaan Kaur, Vice Principal – DHS! Sounds good to you, Mr. Head Boy?"

"Well, it kinda does. No harm really, although I might just end up becoming the *second* Head Boy, thanks to the fact that she is head-over-heels about Jai."

"Huh! Who cares a fuck about him?" Sahana sounded bitchy. "*Chutiya hai woh!"* she added.

Rishav smiled.

Silence again.

"You know, the Council is full of show offs?" Rishav started talking.

"Huh? Like really, what's with your obsession with the Council and the school and its stupid politics? Get a life... Sen! Can we really not talk about this? Please?" irritation for Sahana, often came out of nowhere.

Rishav shrugged, "Yeah sure. So what should we discuss?"

"Umm.... what we are doing today!" came a quick reply.

"And that is?" he asked.

"Going to Connaught Place!"

"Oh yes, sure. Let's talk about Connaught Place!" Rishav mocked.

"Not about Connaught Place, you dumbass! Let's talk about what we are *going* to do there."

"Why of course, we'll do what Princess Sahana loves doing: eating and then shopping. And once that is done, we'll eat a little more. *Hai na?*"

Sahana pinched him. He winced out in pain. Some people turned to look at them.

"First, travel in the General compartment and then have sweaty men around you – stinking like pigs. And add to that your crap – God, give me a break," She cried out of frustration.

Rishav laughed seeing her that way. "You forgot your PDA," he added.

"PDA? What the fuck? I am not showing you any affection by pinching you."

"PDA stands for Public Display of Anger, you idiot!"

"Stop being lame, alright? Like please?" she disdainfully spoke. "And also, stand a little away from me. You creep me out, stop sticking to me in public."

Oh God! Rishav sighed and took a few steps back. Unknowingly, he hit a man, who stood asleep – right behind him. He woke up with the push. "*Kya hai abbe?"* he spoke in a heavy accent presumably from Haryana or Punjab.

Rishav, seeing his size, quickly mustered some readymade apologies as Sahana giggled from a distance.

Life I tell you, he said to himself and badly waited for the train to come halt at the Connaught Place Metro Station.

TWENTY-ONE

"Muskaan madam is the Vice Principal?" the Physics HOD, Suraj Singh spoke in a tone that displayed an amalgamated version of shock and despair. "Help me oh, Newton!" he exclaimed out loud.

He read his text message a number of times to confirm the news. He got up, all anxious. He paced the expanse of his Physics lab.

Midget sized with a disproportionately large skull and the weirdest accent ever – Suraj Singh or 'Pocket Singh' as he was called was happily *sexting* one of his three wives when this horror of an sms came by. His Romanian wife had delivered a baby boy recently and was named Isaac. Suraj Singh's Indian wife had a son named Albert, all that remained was the French one to deliver a kid named Pasteur. Leaving the family matters aside, muttering stuff like: *the equation of motion* and *pendulum,* Suraj Singh raced towards Veenu Sharma's office. He had to score brownie points and now was the time to do so.

He scratched his underarms as he passed the corridors. A bunch of students brushed past him, one of them screamed out – *Pocket Singh*. As though a Suraj Singh in distraught was not enough, the word *Pocket* insulted him like crazy. "Come here!" he ordered.

The boy walked up to him obediently. In a single movement of his hand, Suraj ripped apart the boy's externally stitched pocket. The boy looked at him in awe and disbelief, he had finally been violated by the Pocket Singh and it was a day of celebration for him. "Go now," Suraj instructed.

All smiles, the boy turned around to leave when a voice beckoned Suraj.

"Tearing pockets?" Veenu Sharma stood there, a phone on one hand and her purse on the other.

"Ma'am, ma'am…" Suraj started mumbling.

"What ma'am, ma'am? Go ahead…" she went 'bow-wow' at him.

"I was *zust* trying to…" Suraj was at a loss of words. He was caught red handed.

"Okay, leave that," Veenu said. "Come here…" she ordered.

Suraj quickly walked up to Veenu and positioned himself like an efficient lieutenant.

"Z*i* ma'am?" he asked.

"There is no teacher covering the 11th Commerce Section. Go cover the class instead of tearing pockets."

"Ma'am, but I had to ask you something."

"Your questions aren't important anyway, so just go and do as you are told."

Poor Pocket Singh, one expected a grander recognition of his exploits. And all he got in return was an order to cover a class, "*logarithmic A upon B*," he muttered under his breath as he walked towards Siddhant Dalvi's Commerce section.

"Wanna miss the Library period?" Rishav asked a deeply irritated Sahana, who was restless because the Economics teacher kept on avoiding her perpetually raised hand.

'*What is deficit financing?*' the Eco teacher had asked. And as expected almost three-fourths of the class had no clue about it. But unlike the rest, Sahana Vajpai did. And hell she was angry when she was constantly being denied a chance to rant out the answer to deficit financing.

The teacher looked at her once, twice, thrice but never recognized her to stand up and answer. Sahana remained persistent with her efforts.

Only after the fourth or the fifth look did the teacher, who by the way too, was irritated – recognized Sahana. "Yes Sahana. Please tell us why are you so hyperactive?"

"Ma'am?" Sahana raised an eyebrow and moved her neck a bit.

As she shifted her weight from foot to foot, the teacher commented, "Why are you so restless? Stand in one place first."

Sahana looked on. "Do you want an invitation to speak?" the teacher followed up.

Sahana got weirded out by the lady's constant comments, "Ma'am, I was going to speak but you raised a point about me being hyperactive and erm...restless."

"Yeah, so? Can't I say that?" came the rebuttal.

"Absolutely ma'am. But I don't see how deficit financing is involved..."

"Okay okay, tell me the answer quick," she instructed.

"Ma'am, erm…deficit financing is you know when the RBI, you know…ah, prints excess currency notes to meet the deficit, you know and it leads to a sharp fall in the price of the currency." Sahana said.

"Why do you stutter so much?" The teacher asked. "What is deficit? And who asked you to say what happens when deficit financing is done? You could have just left it to what it is and not what happens."

Oh c'mon bitch, Sahana said to herself. *Get a life woman, personal comments and then follow it up with your feedback!*

"Sit down, anyone else wants to add anything?" the teacher floated another question.

Rishav quickly turned around to face Sahana. She was red with anger, she rolled her eyes. Rishav knew how she must have been abusing the teacher in her head now.

"Calm down," he whispered. He repeated his question, "Want to hang around in the library period?"

Sahana pushed her hair behind her ears, "Yeah sure. But won't our names come up in the log book?"

Rishav thought for two seconds, "We'll tell the logbook incharge not to note it down. What say?"

"Sounds cool," Sahana replied. "What do you want to do?" she asked.

"Open the windows and let some *oxyzen* come in," instructed Suraj Singh who pronounced the syllable 'g' with great difficulty.

The students controlled their laughter. It was funny the way Pocket Singh said things. The intonation, the pronunciation and his whole appearance, made matters worse.

"You know *oxyzen rezuvinates* your body...!" he declared. Siddhant scoffed on hearing this.

Unfortunately for him, Suraj spotted him with ease.

The last thing you'd want is to piss Suraj off when he's giving one of his enlightening statements. He walked towards Siddhant and stood right under his nose.

"Stand up!" Suraj shouted.

Siddhant stood up without any protest.

"What's your name?" he squeaked.

"Sir, Siddhant! Siddhant Dalvi," came the reply.

"Siddhant Dalvi, what do you think of yourself?" Suraj asked.

There were names being called out in the background, in hush voices, the name *Aam chutiya* could be heard very clearly.

"SILENCE!" bellowed Suraj. "Yes, carry on..." he looked at Siddhant.

"Sir, I just scoffed. I didn't laugh at you," he replied with a straight face.

"You *zust* scoffed? What do you think I am a fool?" with a single movement, Siddhant's pocket was now in Suraj's hand.

"Sir, that shirt costs money. How dare you tear my pocket?" Siddhant sounded assertive.

"Aaah, arrogance! First mock a teacher and then reply back," Suraj Singh rolled up his sleeves. He caught hold of the opening of Siddhant's shirt and with a mighty heave, ripped open all his buttons.

Siddhant tried to protest but his strength was nothing when compared to Suraj Singh's. Suraj dragged Siddhant out of his seat, holding him by his buttonless shirt.

The class was silent. None spoke. Even those who were making fun of Siddhant sat speechless, seeing the treatment being handed out to him.

There was a loud noise of Suraj Singh's heavy hand falling on Siddhant's face. "You shall never dare to scoff at me again!" he hissed.

Then came another loud thud on the other side of the face. "You left me no option but to use my hands you arrogant punk."

Siddhant feebly tried to say something like *sorry* when Suraj's left hand landed hard on his face again. It was burning red by now. Suraj Singh then caught him by his sidelocks and dragged him across the expanse of the classroom. He caught hold of Siddhant's hand and twisted it behind his back, Siddhant winced out in pain. "You bloody scum, *tujhe mera aukaat dikhata hu*." Then he followed it up with a few more rights and left and then finally he pushed Siddhant out of his class.

There weren't any cuts on Siddhant's face but he was bruised badly. His face was blued in places, his hair disheveled, his shirt ripped apart and a swollen lip. He fell to the floor and started sobbing. His face hurt badly and his hands were all numb. Suraj closed the door on his face and went back into the class leaving Siddhant all by himself.

TWENTY-TWO

Rishav and Sahana sat near the entrance of their empty classroom. To sit in a class where the clitter clatter of the desks moving was missing, the students laughing out at random things weren't present and the teachers were not trying hard to keep things in check, felt weird. They had become so used to all of it that a brief moment without it felt like something integral was missing.

They were talking about all that they would do when they entered college. It'd be a new place, new people, almost everything would be new. And you could be anything you wanted to. A geek could be a stud; a rich spoilt one could be the uncool one. The girl with the braces could be the hottie; the fat guy could easily be the hunk.

It was a place to start afresh. To undo all wrong that you did in school, to be something you always wished to be, to be a new you.

But then going to school had its own charm. The assemblies, the bunks, the periods and the wait for the moment the bell would ring so that one could rush out of class and gang around in the corridors would all be missed by each and everyone.

Class eleventh would end very soon and thus it'd initiate the beginning of the end of a journey that had lasted almost every one- fourteen years.

Rishav had pulled a chair next to Sahana and their knees were slightly brushing against each other's.

The touch of her skin made Rishav conscious of himself. He was careful not to move his knee too much in case he lost contact. It was the first time that they had been sitting so close and Sahana didn't move away immediately. There was this urge to kiss her, to hold her close and tell her that he loved her. Rishav felt the warmth of Sahana's skin; it was triggering off all kinds of chemical reactions in his body. All he wanted to do was hold her hands and just as his hands were crawling up to hers – they heard footsteps. Sahana immediately pushed her chair back.

A head peeped into the classroom, "Rishav, right?" the boy asked in a tone of urgency.

"Yes, yes, I am Rishav," he said. Sahana turned to look at the boy. He was someone from Vanya's class.

"Come quick," the boy said. "Why?"

"Your friend, Siddhant needs your help!"

"What? *Kya hua?*" Rishav asked. "Just come, okay?" saying this, the boy turned around and made a dash for his section.

"Sahana, wait here, I'll be back," Rishav Sen made his way across the hallway towards the Commerce sections.

Muskaan Kaur studied Siddhant carefully. She narrowed her eyebrows and peered deep into Siddhant's eyes. Hers were as cold as it could get, they contained no expression other than that of spite and hatred towards any student who she deemed to be unfit of being a *Delhite.*

"You scoffed at one of the members of my staff? How dare you?" she said.

Siddhant chose to remain silent. Even speaking hurt his jaws. *Why the fuck doesn't this lady get that?* He said to himself.

Suraj Singh stood at one corner of Muskaan's palatial room, hands on his hips – displaying great quantities of mock indignation. It was like one of those famous Hindi lines, *kuch bhi karne ka lekin Suraj Singh ka ego hurt nahin karne ka!*

Muskaan walked in exact concentric circles around Siddhant while she delivered a monologue on how important it was to respect 'her' staff.

"I got beaten up ma'am," Siddhant protested.

"Well you deserved it!" "You think you could get away by being bold enough to scoff at a respected teacher? You are a moron and you rightfully deserve this treatment. I don't want you to whine to every other teacher about how badly you were beaten. Is that clear?"

Yeah right, Siddhant thought.

"I want to hear it loud and clear Dalvi. You are not supposed to go and whine alright? You should know I have a lot of influence in this Managing Committee and Suraj has the right phone numbers in his contact list. You better be careful next time if you don't want to jeopardize your career."

Siddhant wanted to scream out in frustration. He wanted to tell them how big cunts they were but all that he managed was a faint *yes ma'am.*

Suraj Singh chuckled.

"You may leave Siddhant, Suraj can I have a word with you in private?" she asked.

"*Zi* Ma'am, why not? Sure," he replied courteously.

As Siddhant turned the door knob, Suraj, who was within his hearing range hissed something that sounded similar to 'aam-chutiya'. Siddhant turned a deaf ear and silently walked out.

Jai Chauhan smirked his way to the Physics laboratory. He found Suraj Singh sitting in one corner instructing a few students about how to go about verifying the Ohm's Law. In between he was also making mentions of how he knew the bra sizes of X and Y heroines in the Telegu Film Industry.

"Morning sir," Jai said.

"Mourning *beta,* mourning...not *morning!*" Suraj replied letting out a deep breath of air.

"Hahaha...I heard what you did to that nut. Good one sir!"

Suraj flashed a lopsided grin, "Thank you *beta* – it wasn't a big deal at all."

"Won't his parents complain or anything?" Jai inquired.

"Arre *nahin nahin,* his dad has been dead for years now and his mom runs a small restaurant. They won't want to get into this mess you know."

"His mom runs a small restaurant? Wow. She paid a handsome ten thousand bucks for Socialact Wave yaa!" Jai exclaimed. "Surprising to know about this..."

Suraj interrupted, "Besides that, Muskaan ma'am has issued an order of suspension against Siddhant for fighting in the school premises. We've noted that these bruises are a cause of that."

"Students sir? Students...? They saw it all happen. The entire school knows," Jai replied.

"Yes indeed. They also know the big people I have association with. They will not utter a word against me. *Dekh liyo.*"

Jai nodded. He admired Suraj's guts. "Bindu ma'am knows about this?"

"Of course she does. She knows how I stopped this fight from happening and Veenu is busy fixing her makeup, she took a half day and left and she'll be back only tomorrow and then be off again," he chuckled.

Silence descended upon them for a few seconds till Jai broke it. "You've got a problem sir."

Suraj looked at him urging him to finish his sentence.

"Sir, there's the dick-Head Boy, Rishav. He is Siddhant's best friend, he's got a lot of support from teachers. If he manages to make people rally around..."

Jai was cut short, "*If* he *manazes* naa? That won't happen. I've heard how people find him arrogant and how your peers dislike him. He won't be able to do anything about it. Trust me and if he does, I will manage."

"Sir you will?" Jai's eyes lit up with a lot of interest.

"Yes, yes, I will..."

"Sir, if he *does* complain against you – can you ensure that he's stripped off his post?" Jai asked again.

"Stripped? I can get him off from his post for sure but I don't have any idea how long. You see, that power lies with the Prinicpal alone."

Jai nodded.

Jai had to meet Rishav. He had to meet him...*now!*

TWENTY-THREE

Veenu Sharma had taken a half day without notice and she was perhaps the only person Rishav Sen eagerly wanted to meet.

He clumsily packed his bag and zipped it up fast. The bell had just rung ending the day and it was his only chance to catch the Principal while she was doing her rounds.

Autocracy that seemed to be the only mode of functioning, as far as Bindu Kalsi was concerned- seemed to have gone for a six in Delhi High School as the well informed Principal had now become a titular head. Muskaan Kaur was dictating the terms to all and sundry.

The image of a sobbing Siddhant had moved Rishav tremendously. He felt it to be his duty to be helping that loner out. Besides most teachers were unaware of the atrocities that took place within the walls of the Commerce section last day and those who knew – be it students or teachers were all too afraid of Suraj Singh to be exposing him. And the person who was supposed to be aware of all the happenings, the Principal was lost in her own world: too busy in organizing Socialact Wave.

Rishav thought of all that Jai had told him. Jai seemed to be a nice person, he encouraged Rishav to take a stand and visit Muskaan Ma'am. Jai insisted on how Rishav should drive his point across by hook or by crook. After all, it was a matter of the students' unity.

Little did Rishav know that Jai's encouragement was a façade over his true intentions.

In moments, Rishav spotted Kalsi's figure standing outside the entrance to the Multipurpose Hall. She was engaged in deep discussion with someone Rishav would have killed to not see there – Muskaan!

"Yes?" Kalsi asked seeing Rishav approach them.

"Ma'am I need to talk about something." He said.

"Go on..." she replied.

"Ma'am, erm...uh...I need to speak to you," he stammered.

"I wonder if there's anything as urgent that cannot be discussed with me?" Muskaan asked.

"No ma'am, it is. I need to speak to the Principal."

Muskaan broke into a fake laughter, Kalsi followed.

"It is okay Rishav, you can speak to Muskaan. I have pressing matters right now." Kalsi said.

"No Ma'am, I need to talk to you," he insisted.

"It is okay son, Muskaan is *me*, speak to her. She will tell me whatever needs to be relayed."

"That's it then," she said when she heard what Rishav had done.

"What? What do you mean?" he asked.

"We are done," Sahana repeated in a dead serious tone.

He tried to come closer, but Sahana pushed him back vehemently.

"What the fuck are you doing, you son of a bitch? Stay away, *forever.* And I am not kidding," she shouted out loud in the empty classroom they were sitting in.

"What the hell is wrong with you Sahana? Can't you for once understand my position?" Rishav said defensively.

"Oh yes, baby. I have," she said in a conspicuous sarcastic voice. "I have understood your point. Your position, it's all crystal clear to me."

She paused and took a deep breath, "You bloody bastard. All you care about is your *effing* position. Your ugly piece of metal…And you know what? You are the biggest hypocrite in this whole world. The biggest. I actually cannot think of an abuse worthy enough for you."

Rishav was hurt. Badly hurt. He felt his anger burn up his insides but he tried to control it.

"You don't know what it's like, okay?" he began. "You bloody haven't even talked to them. You don't even own a badge. What would you know about how it feels to lose it? Well, you are the hypocrite here, not me. You bloody didn't have the balls to even apply for the Council. So shut the fuck up. You just say things and never actually do it. So, please save me the crap. All your moral talk is of no freaking use, get it?" Rishav screamed, laying emphasis on the last words.

Sahana stood her ground, slightly taken aback.

"You know what Rishav? You are right," she said in a cold tone. Her voice barely a whisper, "You are right, I don't. But, atleast I don't pretend to be someone I am not. Jai Chauhan is actually better than you. Atleast he doesn't *pretend* to be good."

"Sahana, listen...I don't want to fight. So please, can we not talk about it?" Rishav asked, afraid that Sahana would leave his side.

"Yes, I don't want to fight. But I can't stand your face. Don't you dare come near me ever again," Sahana said.

"Sahana please. I am sorry. Don't do this over a stupid thing, Rishav said trying to hold Sahana's hand.

"Go fuck yourself," Sahana said in his ear as she pushed him against the classroom door and stormed out of there.

Rishav lay in his bed, unable to sleep. It was two in the morning and he couldn't even get a wink of sleep. All he could think about was what happened that day.

To say it was the worst day ever, would be a massive understatement. He had lost the only two people he cared about.

Firstly, Siddhant – who he had not lost exactly but not standing up for him and agreeing to turn a blind eye over a wrong thing, was all in all, a betrayal of sorts. Secondly, he couldn't figure out what was it that he felt for Sahana. It was deep nonetheless but it was hard to understand what it was in reality. He had never in his life felt this way before. The thought of not talking to her, scared him. But now the thought of even seeing her was a distant dream. As much as he missed her, he was frustrated with her attitude. She couldn't even understand his point of view. All she cared was about her principles. She was yet to know the difference between the real world and an idealistic one she lived in, he thought.

He tried to think of something else. But nothing would come to his mind except that he had lost the two people who mattered to him the most. He looked down at the badge he was holding tightly in his palms: **Head Boy: Rishav Sen,** it read.

He held it in the palm of his hand & shut his eyes.

TWENTY-FOUR

Rishav was late to school. He had woken up just fifteen minutes before school actually started. He didn't bother to apply soap on his body. *What's the use?* He thought as he quickly poured water over his body.

The guard let him in with a smile, since he knew very well who the Head Boy was. He had told Rishav about his village, his problems, his children's schooling, his daughter's favourite movie and what not. Rishav had not spared one man in DIIS with his charm and good talks.

He rushed to his class with heavy steps. He walked towards his seat in the half empty classroom but stopped midway to think, *it'd be better not to sit in Sahana's range.*

He chose a far cornered seat in the classroom as he had enough of a choice that day.

He took out his mobile and checked his inbox. **No Unread Messages**. He looked at his mobile with disdain. He went to check his Facebook, **No New Notifications**. When he turned on his Gmail, he saw an unread message from his publisher, reminding him about the deadline for submitting the manuscript of his third to-be-bestseller. He also noticed a few fan mails and some newsletters.

Rishav read all the fan mails in his inbox. He always felt good when he did that. It gave him the satisfaction that people still cared. When he looked up from his mobile screen, he noticed that the class was now almost empty as all had left for the library.

He got up and walked towards the library alone. As he walked through the corridors, he remembered the first day of school. It was all a big maze but now he knew every corner of it. Eight months seemed to have flown by just so quickly.

In the library, he took a newspaper and sat alone on a deserted table. He scanned the two floored library, he noticed things he seemed to have never noticed before. Like, he had never noticed the painting hanging on the wall or the door to the small terrace above, or the replica of the Eiffel tower sitting on one of the tables. He looked at all the people sitting nearby. It was a joint library period with the Commerce stream. Siddhant was nowhere to be seen, *good for him*, Rishav thought. Surprisingly, Sahana too was missing.

After the end of the period, he walked back from the library to the classroom – alone, yet again. He entered the classroom and saw Sahana and Vanya sitting together. Vanya's constant detours to their classroom had begun to bother Rishav but he chose not to say anything about it.

He felt a pain stretching his arteries. He wanted to go talk to Sahana. But after a lot of consideration, he decided against it. He knew heart in heart that giving her time, enough to think about it was the best thing he could do.

Just when he was about to resume wasting his time on his

mobile phone, an announcement on the PA system caught his attention.

'This message is for all Council members. Please report to the outer-stage for the final run through of the Socialact Wave.'

He sighed, he knew that with the event being just around the corner – he'd be required to do a lot of running around. He geared up for it and dragged himself out of the class reluctantly.

It was six in the evening by the time, the final preparations for Socialact Wave finally winded up. The event was scheduled to be held in a couple of days and the sponsors had already poured in whatever money they had to. On the gala dress rehearsal that day, everyone was pretty high and most Socialact Club members were swimming in a pool of Vodka. It was like the party was yet to begin but the lead up to it had to be as exciting as it could be. They all headed to a famous hookah bar close by to enjoy the success of putting together one of the most tainted functions to have been ever organized in the history of the school.

Jai and his gang walked around backslapping the random Delhite when Jai's Blackberry beeped. He had subscribed to the Delhi High School group page on Facebook. He smartly maneuvered his fingers to reach the link to that page. He read the update and couldn't quite believe what he saw. He read it again.

He turned to Chintan, "Dude, this must be some kind of a prank. Just check any alternate group page of Delhi High School, please?"

"Sure," Chintan said and started fiddling with his Blackberry. In matter of minutes, Chintan's jaw dropped.

"What the fuck man?" he yelped. Hardik who was right behind

them got interested too and in just about minutes, his Blackberry beeped too.

None out of Chintan, Hardik or Jai could believe what they were seeing but they had no other option but to go there and verify.

After a long hard day of getting ordered by the members of the teaching staff, Rishav ambled across the hallway to reach the Reception Area of Delhi High School. He least expected it to be crowded especially it being the beginning of the long week when Wave would be held – it was a time when people would be preserving their energies for the main event as the organizing was already done. As he moved closer towards the Reception door, he heard loud voices. There was indeed a crowd gathered around there.

What luck! Rishav thought. Just when he was thinking of untucking his shirt and loosening his tie, he comes across a crowd in the Reception area. And generally a crowd in the Reception Area consisted of outsiders and no Council Member was allowed to be in improper uniform around that place.

He saw Veenu Sharma who apparently seemed to be crying. Bindu Kalsi sat nearby wearing a contemplative look while Muskaan Kaur paced the area around her. Besides them, there were around thirty other staff members sitting at different locations. Suraj Singh seemed to have attracted an abnormal number of them.

Rishav quickened his pace and walked straight upto Veenu Sharma, not caring a hoot about whether his actions would be dissected or not.

"Ma'am?" he asked politely.

She looked up. "What's wrong ma'am? What is everyone doing here so late? Why are you crying?" there were so many questions in his head.

"Didn't you hear?" Veenu Sharma asked in between sobs.

"What ma'am?" Rishav was dumbstruck.

"Your friend, Siddhant…Siddhant Dalvi jumped off the roof of his house. He's dead." She said.

Rishav looked on in total disbelief. He remained silent for a minute or so and then finally, he felt his world come crashing down on him.

TWENTY-FIVE

Rishav slipped through the mass of white clothes and sad faces.

"Excuse me," he said as he raised his hands over his head and tried to squeeze his lanky frame past the last of the mourners. As he went closer to the body, Rishav's eyes widened in horror as Veenu Sharma's words finally seemed to have struck him.

Fully draped in white, the body of Rishav's first friend in Delhi High School lay there peacefully. Siddhant Dalvi. Siddhant appeared even more serene in death than what he was in reality. There seemed to be no inkling of the trauma that he had been subjected to prior to his death. The only signs that lay testament to his horror were the bruise marks all over his face that he had received at the hands of Suraj Singh. His mother sat right beside him, crying her heart out as some of their relatives tried consoling her.

Rishav stood there for a moment, blankly staring at the lifeless Siddhant. He was too shocked to even cry. It seemed just about a couple of days back when he had met a shaken Siddhant after the Suraj episode. Even then, Siddhant refused to divulge any details of the brutal assault; such was his commitment towards the school and the whole idea of its image being untarnished. Siddhant's laughter echoed in his ears. It seemed ages since he last heard it, how he wished that he had spent more memorable moments with Siddhant. He wished that as friends, he had more chances to bright up Siddhant's face with a smile. He looked on as the first traces of tears rolled down his eyes.

He remembered his first day in school and Siddhant's move forward. He remembered being shown around the school and being told about its hypocrisies and double standards. It was ironical that the one who saw through all the superficiality was the one who had to end his life. It was ironical that Suraj Singh would soon be promoted to an administrative position.

Rishav shifted his long gaze from the body to his surroundings. He saw a number of familiar faces, including those who never cared for Siddhant when he was alive.

"How did you know him?" a man in his mid-40s asked Rishav politely.

"I am his friend from school," he replied. "Rishav Sen, that's my name."

Rishav noticed the man's expression change, "Oh yes, Siddhant spoke of you a lot. He was all praises about how you managed so well in a changing environment."

Rishav barely smiled as the man spoke, "I am his maternal uncle."

Rishav nodded, mumbling a faint, "Nice to meet you Sir."

It seemed that the effect of Siddhant's death had totally sunk in for his uncle. The gentleman seemed abnormally stable at the time of such a tragic moment. Some amounts of silence prevailed between the two, till the person broke it.

"He was very polite to his elders, he worshipped his teachers really. I wonder how he got into that fight," he said.

It was hard to believe that Siddhant's family was yet to know the real reason of the bruises that he had got in school. Or the real reason why he died, though Rishav didn't know much about it either.

"I know it's not the right moment to ask Sir, but erm...by any chance did Siddhant leave behind a note or something. Huh?" Rishav asked hesitantly.

The gentleman rummaged his pockets and took out a crumbled piece of paper, "I had to hide it from my sister." He said, "It'd be great, if you don't tell anyone we found this." He stuffed the piece of paper into Rishav's open palms in a hurry, lest somebody saw it.

"I have to make a move and organize for the ambulance that will take him to the crematorium," the man said.

"He will be cremated today?" Rishav asked as he spent a minute straightening out the crumbled piece of paper. By the time he looked up to expect an answer, Siddhant's uncle was gone.

Siddhant Dalvi sat on a wall...
Siddhant Dalvi had a great fall...
All the world's horses & all the world's friends...
Couldn't put Dalvi together again...

This is gonna be the last time I'll ever be touching a sketch pen, You know why??

...cuz I am gonnaa jump!!

Yeah, you heard it right, I wanna jump. It's got nothing to do with the fact that I'm drunk. Just randomly I wanna experience what Batman does.

I have had enough of life actually, that's the reason I want to taste some thrill. Noone cares if I freaking live or not. I am really trying to make sense but you know what? I don't have prior experience of writing suicide notes so please don't make fun of the aam-chutiya after he's gone? Alright?

I'll miss my moter, I know heaven can never afford a creature as beautiful as her. And well, aaaah...leave it...I am disoriented and I dont have time really. So goodbye world.

Remember me in death cuz you've never been able to remember me while I was alive.

SidDal

Siddhant was void of a lot of things in his lifetime but what hurt Rishav the most was the fact that Siddhant always deserved more than what he got but he seldom complained. Siddhant was content and his death would turn out to be the decisive moment in someone's life – Rishav Sen would finally get to feel the presence of a spine.

Bindu Kalsi grabbed the folder lying closest to her and flung it across the room in a fit of rage. It crashed into the flower vase that adorned the bookshelf right in front of her.

Even before the sound of the class vase shattering into pieces could die down, she screamed out, "You morons did not tell me that Suraj had beaten up the Dalvi boy?"

Muskaan Kaur and Neeti Chopra stood silent, with their heads down like little school kids did when they were reprimanded by their teachers.

"And Muskaan, you had the audacity to write a false suspension letter? Under what pretext?" Kalsi shouted.

"BK..." Muskaan began.

Kalsi interrupted her, "And remember this, when you are addressing me, you are addressing this *office*, so I want to hear the word - *ma'am,* the next time you speak."

Muskaan Kaur gulped her ego down the long esophagus and spoke again. "Ma'am," she began. "What was done was done in the best interests of this institution, if news of Dalvi getting assaulted by a teacher was to be made public, it would only harm the school's reputation and in a way, *your* reputation."

Fumes came out of Kalsi's nostrils as Muskaan continued.

"People fear Suraj Singh, not a single student will speak up against him. Do be rest assured about that and I got information that Dalvi boy was drunk when he died."

Kalsi stopped fuming, "He was drunk?" She asked. "Who told you?"

"My sources," replied Muskaan.

"Your sources?" Kalsi guffawed.

"From amongst those present at Dalvi's funeral," Muskaan added.

"Hmmm..." Kalsi nodded. "What's the course of action then?"

"Simple, we stick by our official stand. Siddhant Dalvi was involved in a brawl and we add to that some family issues that drove him to commit suicide."

"His father was the senior peon of our school for long. He even served my father, Mr. Chavan. We can't do this to a DHS loyalist, we can't defame his son," Kalsi pronounced.

"Then you decide for yourself. What is more important to you – the reputation of your school and you or the image of a dead boy," Muskaan smirked.

Kalsi remained silent for a while, "Fine, I trust your judgment. But this will be one final time, promise me Muskaan, you shall not take things into your own hands like this...*ever again*."

"Yes, yes, for sure," Muskaan replied in a hurry. "Now let's talk about some other pressing matters, Socialact Wave, who are you inviting as the Chief Guest?" she asked.

Kalsi who was sipping her steaming cup of coffee, choked all of a sudden. "Socialact Wave?" she asked.

Both Neeti and Muskaan nodded.

"Are you sure we should host something like this? Right after the death of one of our students?"

"He's dead *na*...." Muskaan replied. "Why do you want it to lay any bearing on what we do with one of the biggest events in our school calendar? Aren't you forgetting our commitments to our sponsors and all the people like Veer Chauhan, who've donated so generously?"

Kalsi didn't speak which gave Muskaan further incentive to go on, "Our official stand rubbishes the claim that Dalvi was beaten up by one of the members of our staff. So let's not try being over-sensitive, alright? Socialact Wave goes on as planned."

"I have my doubts Muskaan, surely the sponsors can be told that the event has been postponed?" Kalsi enquired.

"No, they cannot," Muskaan seemed to have lost control and in an impulse spoke loudly.

Kalsi turned to face the large glass window overlooking her lawn. She slowly turned to face the two ladies again. "Fine, Socialact Wave would be on as scheduled. Now for God's sake, let me finish my cup of coffee in peace."

Neeti and Muskaan took their final bows and quietly walked out of the office. Kalsi ensured that her phone was off the hook. She pushed back her chair and enjoyed little sips of the hot drink.

It seemed the story of Siddhant Dalvi was disappearing just like those wisps of steam coming out of her cup and vanishing in thin air.

TWENTY-SIX

Suraj Singh was in between one of his routine discussions on the actual value of pie when a phone call diverted his attention. "*Escuse* me children," he said, as he moved to one corner of the class to receive the phone.

"*Zi* Muskaan madam?" he asked.

"Why aren't you in my office yet?" she demanded an answer.

"Ma'am, extremely sorry ma'am. But I didn't get the message." He silently waited for her reply.

"I don't care, if you love your job, I want to see you here in thirty seconds," she curtly said before hanging up.

A phone call from Muskaan Kaur did what years of orders from Singhal and Kalsi couldn't do – it sent alarm bells ringing in Suraj's head.

Without much ado and without telling a soul about where he was going and why was he leaving the class halfway, Suraj Singh made a dash for Muskaan's office.

In about a couple of minutes, when he finally reached, he found the office to be abnormally crowded. Class representatives of all classes in the Senior Wing had gathered around the small coffee table that stood in one corner of Muskaan's room (Madhuri's old room).

"Come in quick," Muskaan said, gently rotating her chair from right to left.

The other teachers who were already inside the room were discussing things in hush voices but on seeing Suraj, all of them fell silent. Now the attention moved towards the lady in the green saree.

"As you may know," Muskaan began. "We have a problem. And the solution to the problem lies in successfully organizing Socialact Wave." This was followed by some murmurs that died down as soon as they started.

"Siddhant Dalvi's death has shaken up the Principal," she coughed. "And we all know who is responsible for it," she looked at Suraj. "Nevertheless, I need to ensure that there is no unnecessary gossiping and wastage of time going on in this school because..." she got up from her seat and adjusted her saree. She sat down again, "the last thing I want is a God damn *revolution* in this school." She clenched her teeth as she said it. "Is it understood?"

Everyone nodded. So, now we have the instructions for you, "There will be no subject teaching for the next couple of days till Wave officially gets over. The home-room teacher will stay with the students all day and ensure that none and when I say none, I mean none, is allowed to leave the classroom for any reason whatsoever." Some more murmurs as she prepared to speak again, "It is a very sensitive situation for us right now, the Press will gobble us up if they get to know about this and any kind of new found unity amongst students will be catastrophic. Get the priorities straight, Socialact Wave is more important than your blessed lives."

The teachers turned to face Ashish Dutta, the senior-most and the most respected teacher in the senior school. He weighed his words before he spoke, "Madam, I feel it is more advisable that we take some kind of action against Suraj..."

Suraj Singh got agitated on hearing this. So agitated that he shouted out an expletive, "What the hell *bhenchod,* Ashish *bhai, yeh tum kya keh rahe ho*?"

"What I say is correct, the outcome maybe worse you know? If we take some action against Suraj it will kill any kind of rebellious act that we are expecting..."

"Tch tch tch...Ashish, do as you are said. Please, my dear?" Muskaan pleaded in fakeness.

Ashish fell silent. "Is that all?" Muskaan asked.

The teachers were in a dilemma, they didn't want to ask unnecessary questions and piss Muskaan off. On the other hand they knew how strenuous and crap-like it'd be to sit in class all day and be a watchdog for the students. Eventually, everyone agreed on principle that Muskaan's instructions were worth being followed and they left her room like obedient school children.

Runjhun Sharma was having her usual hectic day at work in the clumsily built office of DNN-IGN News Agency, when her phone rang.

A journalist's life was never void of phone calls and people who seldom understood the idea of 'beats' appeared to be the ones who'd call incessantly. At times the calls would be desirable, like information for really interesting stories that could grab a huge number of eyeballs while, at times the calls would be that of a lack-in-life call centre guy, ever readily wanting to get abused.

Runjhun generally took charge of the Lifestyle and Entertainment Beat and when at times there was a dearth of journalists, she would be asked to take care of the Literature section too.

Strangely, the past few weeks had been mellow by her standards. There were lesser number of phone calls: wanted and unwanted. The Editor seemed to be in a chirpier mood, her love life had taken a plunge and she wasn't getting hold of a single path breaking story that could bring the pandemonium back in her life again. And just when she was thinking of taking the rest of the day off, her phone rang. It was an unknown number but there was hardly any option other than to answer the call and find out the 'mystery' of the caller.

"Hi, Runjhun Sharma, DNN-IGN," she said the moment she picked up the call.

"Hello, erm, Runjhun right?" the voice asked.

"Yeah, that's right. Runjhun, this side," you could feel the smile in her voice.

"Hi Runjhun, I got your number from your sister. I'm Rishav calling from DHS."

"Hey Rishav, no wonder you know my sister, same class?"

"Not really, sections are different," he replied.

"So tell me, how I can be of help to you?" she asked politely.

"See, it's hard to tell it to you on the phone but I'll try to explain it to you as quickly as I can. Ask me if you don't understand anything."

"Go on, I'm all ears..."

"Well, you heard about the recent mishap, the suicide of the DHS student named Siddhant Dalvi?" he enquired.

"Who hasn't? Of course I did, sad thing to hear that he got

drunk, pretty depressing life he had huh?"

"That's not it, that is *not* the story. I've tried telling this to others but there's some kind of restriction imposed in school which is really making it hard to communicate."

"Oh c'mon, it's the age of Facebook, surely you can't sell such excuses," she chuckled.

"It's something serious and perhaps I have too much on my plate already to take a conscious effort into solving this crisis. So I sought help from *real* people with real impact. And it led me to you," he completed.

"That's interesting, so what's the catch?"

"There's a lot of malpractices going on within the walls of DHS and it must be made available to the common public. Also, Dalvi's death wasn't suicide. Even if it was, people are being forced to take it at face value. A couple of days back, Dalvi had been assaulted by a teacher with strong political clouts. School refused to take action against him, that humiliation plus whatever he had sustained all throughout his stay drove Siddhant to a point of insanity. That's what killed him, he jumping off from the roof was just the tip of the iceberg," Rishav sounded exasperated at the end of it.

"I see, but clearly you are in the wrong beat. The crime beat might..." she began.

"No, no. I am in the right beat. It took me long to convince myself to trust you. I can't do it all over again with someone else you see. I know how you can pull off this story without requiring any support from other beats."

"You know? How?"

"Socialact Wave, a largely popular music event will be held day-after. You cover it under entertainment. Then you can write an article on how the school is 'celebrating' the death of a student."

"It sounds interesting, though I am not sure if that'd be enough to make enough of a case against the school."

"Listen to me, I have more really. I can give you details of how alcohol is being provided to inmates of the school hostel- And that too, under the full knowledge of the warden. I can also tell you about how the Principal is deliberately appearing to be unaware of the large scale hypocrisies in and around her. I can provide you with a lot of information, but you first write about how the school doesn't care about its' students, drag in the assault and subsequent suicide of Siddhant. Bring in the lies of the management and the tightlipped stands that stink of double standards," he could rant on and on.

"Okay, okay. Chill dude, what are you, some anti-DHS encyclopedia or something?" she asked.

"No, I am just one pissed off Head Boy, who can chuck his badge a million miles away and never ever think of it."

"What the fish!" Runjhun exclaimed. "You are the Head Boy and you are ready to do all of this?"

"Yeah, I am. Anything for my friend; I will provide you with passes for Socialact Wave. Please, please make sure the story is hard hitting."

"I can't promise anything, you know, it all depends on what my Ed perceives of my story."

"She'll like it," he replied confidently.

"You think so?" she asked.

"I know so," came the reply. "I will get in touch with you day-after. Please do be there, one of those few occasions when you can stand up for a good cause. They don't come everyday in your life."

"I will, I will," saying this, Runjhun Sharma hung up.

TWENTY-SEVEN

The early morning Delhi smog almost engulfed the Delhi High School campus as a lone figure walked past its entrance and was on to the concrete lane that led to the Boys Hostel in almost no time. Once he crossed the glaring eyes of the Hostel warden's security guard, he broke into a sharp jog and moved towards the Hostel entrance.

The elderly caretaker, affectionately called *Bhau* or brother was doing his routine job of knocking on the doors of each and every student, asking them to wake up as it was time for them to go for their morning run.

It was Rishav's second or third visit to the Boy's Hostel but it was the first time he actually got to see the interiors of it. The size of the rooms gave him bouts of claustrophobia and the state of the bathing rooms made him nauseas. *And we complain about our homes?* He said to himself.

Bhau quickly escorted him towards the Warden's office.

"Are you sure, you won't fall into any trouble?" Rishav asked the gingerly old man.

"No, no son, I am immune. They can't dare to touch me even; I have support of the Union. But, then what about you? Are you also a part of the Student Union?" he asked as he moved in short but quick paced steps.

"Council *bhau* not Union and besides, I think I have stepped down, by my actions of course" Rishav replied with a hint of relief in his voice.

"Stepped down? Why?"

"Politics and dirt, it's a long story. You know Siddhant Dalvi?" Rishav inquired.

"Yes, yes, Shekhar Dalvi's son – I saw him being born. Saddened and grieved to hear of his death..."

"Death *nahi Bhau,* murder!" Rishav exclaimed.

"Murder? Are you kidding me?" the old man stroked his pepper-salt stubble.

"Yes, yes, murder. It's a long story *Bhau* but what I need to do right now is enter the Warden's office unnoticed."

"Just a few more steps and you are there," *Bhau* replied.

It was Diwali when Rishav had spotted the old man running around to get an errant done. Not used to coming to that part of the school, he had found it extremely difficult to get his job done. That's when Rishav Sen, at his prime as the Head Boy helped him around by personally showing him around to the right people. "I owe you one," *Bhau* had said to him. It was time Rishav came to seek the favour.

Rishav got to know from his hostel friends that a crate of packed *Queenfisher* beer cans had made its way to the Hostel. Although at the sight of it, it seemed to be a direct slap on the face of the authorities, it was not to be. Each crate which had been ordered by some powerful names in the hostel had a commission of two hundred rupees attached to it. And the entire money was being pocketed by the Warden.

"Twenty five crates came in, last night..." *Bhau* said as he unlocked the door. "Look under the Warden's cupboard," he pointed.

Rishav couldn't believe what he saw. After all the crap he had read about in the school's prospectus, there was something as appalling as liquor being served to minors in the Hostel of a premier institution.

"What do you want to do now?" the old man asked.

"Expose these bastards," Rishav replied.

"I would advise you against it though. You don't want to get thrown out," he said.

"I won't, trust me. You have the receipts signed by the Warden?" Rishav asked.

"Why do you think the Warden would sign them?"

"Because that bastard would want his share of commission," Rishav chuckled.

In the background, the sound of shuffling slippers could be heard. Students were already out of their rooms, making their way towards the mess for their morning glass of milk.

"You are correct, he does have receipts but I don't want you to fall into trouble." *Bhau* insisted.

"Okay, then you have to let me click photographs."

Bhau shook his head in stark disapproval of Rishav's idea. But Rishav Sen continued to relent, till the man allowed him to take out his mobile phone and click some well defined snaps of the murk that existed right under Bindu Kalsi's fat ass!

One for DNN-IGN, cheeeseee! He said under his breath, while he clicked the 'capture' button.

THREE DAYS LATER

TWENTY-EIGHT

If one bothered to peep through the tinted glass panes of Mrs.Bindu Kalsi's office at Delhi High School, it wouldn't be too hard to predict the temperatures out there. The heat was definitely on and that too, on a cold December morning.

In his robust self, the Chairman of the Delhi High School Society paced Kalsi's office, up and down. While, an anxious Kalsi stood, yes, she stood unlike the million times; she'd want to rest her big butt on her comfortable chair. But then, seeing the Chairman so restless had unnerved her to no extent. With those pudgy fingers resting against the wooden table of hers, her eyes followed the Chairman's movements at all times.

Apart from the two of them, Ms. Muskaan was present in the room. She displayed vast quantities of nonchalance by the looks of it, but deep within that cramped heart of hers, she was worried too and the fact that she was referring to the Chairman as *Sir* and not *Chandra ji* stood as evidence to the claim that she was indeed skeptical about what to expect from the imminent signs of danger. The creeper of insecurity was finally making its presence felt in Muskaan Kaur's life.

Chandrashekhar looked at the paper in disbelief; he had been reading and re-reading it since the moment his wife had given it to him that morning. In between his motions, the Chairman was having a jolly good time imagining himself pole dancing with the hottest chicks of tinsel town, but that was clearly not to be. Two knocks on the bathroom door suggested that his sluggish wife had some news for him. Luckily enough for him, she wasn't really demanding him to have sex with her in the bathroom. Rather, it was this newspaper article she wanted him to read. And yes, one roll of his eyes over the article was good enough to shake off the motion-sensations as he sprinted towards the shower to get ready at a speed that would make Usain Bolt look like a tortoise.

Generally, the Chairman was the one who'd keep others waiting but today, he reached half-an-hour ahead of schedule, much to the surprise and shock of everyone. The first thing he noticed after entering was that almost every god damned person was carrying the morning edition of *DNN Times*. And ironically, the headlines for that newspaper seemed to be drawing so much of unnecessary attention that even those who'd be the last ones to sacrifice their morning doze of gossip and *chai* were convinced enough to sacrifice the former and do some 'critical reading'.

There was this article that was prominently displayed on the top half of the newspaper.

CELEBRATING THE *'Boy Who Died'*

Delhi High School hosts its annual extravaganza while family mourns.

By Runjhun Sharma, DNN-IGN

New Delhi: The much acclaimed and coveted Delhi High School recently hosted its annual musical extravaganza – *Socialact Wave* in the school grounds on Tuesday. Apart from being an eyeball grabber, the event boasted of a lot of undeserved hype and attention. Funded by the Boating Club of India and passionately sponsored by Mr.Veer Chauhan, the Socialact Club organized this event like it does, every year. However, after the arrival of Mrs.Bindu Kalsi, who took over as the Principal, April this year – the school has witnessed some overhauling changes. One of the major noticeable changes has been the shift of the venue for the event – Socialact Wave which used to take place in the school auditorium finally got a new venue (which I hear is after a long time) in the form of the school ground. Apart from the overrated performance of the band 'EksCruciate' and long monotonous speeches from the Principal and the Vice Principal, what missed everyone's eyes was the news of the tragic death of a Class XI student of Delhi High School, Siddhant Dalvi. Dalvi (17) had committed what some call suicide in the wee hours of Saturday morning. The school's initial response was that of shock after which it quite smartly shirked off all kinds of responsibility from the event by calling it 'tragic' and saying that it was inevitable as Dalvi was in an inebriated state. What the school has failed to acknowledge is the fact that a number of occurrings happened in the school and are still taking place, which is leading young kids like Dalvi to the brink of ending their life. And much to the hypocrisy of a school which claims to love its family endlessly, the staging of Socialact Wave stands as a fact to the claim that the school is hoodwinking not only its parents but also the society of which it is a part of.

From reports that have been gathered from credible sources, it is learnt that a large consignment of alcohol had entered the school premises through the hostel, some days before Wave. Photos that were captured show that the crates were being stored by the Hostel warden himself and then being released to students on payment of commission. It is no joke that alcohol had been made illegally available to most who sought it during the staging of Socialact Wave. The headbanging and ear-splitting music aside, there were other events. There've been events of greater magnitude than Socialact Wave that each one should be aware of. DNN-IGN has gathered that in the lead-up to Dalvi's suicide, Dalvi had been brutally assaulted by one of the members of the teaching faculty of Delhi High School. There happened to be some kind of confrontation between the student and the teacher which resulted in Dalvi being treated dishonourably and humiliated in front of his peers. As though that wasn't enough, the eleventh grader's shirt was ripped apart by the teacher and he was slapped repeatedly and thrown out of the class. The school's official stand had like usual, been that of denial. The school instead, maligned Dalvi by stating that he was involved in a brawl outside school and also slapped a suspension notice against the kid. However, no action was taken against the staff member for unknown reasons.

DNN-IGN has made repeated attempts to get the comments of top officials of the DHS Society; however, all of them have refused to make any statements. Mrs. Bindu Kalsi, Principal, Delhi High School has kept her phone on silent mode ever since we first tried to contact her. Much to their ignorance, the top officials believed that not being available would deter us from getting this story out. Siddhant Dalvi's close friend and ex-Head Boy, Rishav Sen had spoken to us and he said that the main reason why he had given up his position recently was because he no longer believed in the system. One known figure from the student fraternity did refute our claims and dismissed them as baseless allegation and he was Head Boy, Jai Chauhan, who is also the Secretary of the Socialact Club.

One doesn't really care about Jai but one does want to hear comments from the 'real' people. When will they speak up?

(This report has been published in view of the interest of the general public of the city. The reports are backed by the presence of credible sources).

Chandrashekhar's first reaction on reading such incredible news was what was most expected – the one of shock. But as the shock gradually set into his system, it struck him that he had received no calls from DNN-IGN whatsoever. This in turn made him realize that Kalsi's people from within the organization had deliberately tried to suppress this information from him. So, at that point of time, nothing was more important than going to DHS and sorting the matter out with Kalsi herself.

"I didn't know that it was of such great magnitude," said Kalsi mournfully. "I was mistaken. An honest mistake from my side," she added.

The Chairman shook his head in regret. Muskaan spoke, "Erm, uh, we have contacts in the Ministry, surely we can kill this news? And public memory is short, it won't erm really hamper the school's progress would it?" she stuttered.

The Chairman remained silent. His silence was killing Muskaan and Kalsi.

"Sir, if only you could guide us during this hour of duress like you have had all these years, with your exceptional leadership abilities and…" Kalsi could go on and on.

Chandrashekhar raised a hand and asked her to stop, "Enough Bindu. Enough." He said.

Muskaan looked at him; vary of what he'd say next.

"For all the years I've worked with your father, I have never imagined that a day would come when I'd want to even raise my voice at a member of the Chavan family. But, you have compelled me to," he looked up. "What on holy earth were you thinking?" he shouted. "Why do you have such nincompoops running the entire school, I don't understand." He said a few of the f-words to personify his statement.

Kalsi couldn't dare to reply.

"A child died, add to that a teacher beating him up and going unreported. Then we have Muskaan's crazy insistence and affection towards programs like Wave, do you really want this old man to not live his final years in peace?" he demanded an answer.

The facial muscles of Muskaan twitched when the Chairman mentioned her, "Sir, let me point out that Wave has generated profits of..." typical of Muskaan, the statistics were always so clear in her head.

"To hell with the statistics," screamed Chandrashekhar. "Profits can't buy me back the name of this school. You get me Muskaan?"

"Chandra ji..."

"It's Sir, Muskaan...call me sir."

"Okay," Muskaan gulped down her ego. "Sir," she said. "All that I'm saying is that we haven't lost everything. We can still get a statement out saying how these allegations are false."

"No," he revoked her stand. "You shall do nothing of that sort. From today, all decisions to be taken in this school will be sanctioned by me and I clearly do not sanction this move."

Kalsi and Muskaan nodded hesitantly.

"Did you even read the article? Did you even see how hard hitting it was? And I still can't understand why you chose to hold an event right after the student's death. Why couldn't you wait?"

"The sponsors would run away," mumbled Muskaan.

"A child is dead and all you care about are sponsors? Shame on you Muskaan. Really, unexpected," he replied. Her head bowed down a little.

They remained quiet for a few seconds.

"We need to clear the air; we need to speak to the media." He declared.

"No, we can't do that," replied Kalsi.

"If you can't, then I'll put a new Principal in this room who *can*. So you better not give me this nonsense Bindu," he raised his voice again. "I want you there on National Television clearing the air about this issue. No matter what stand you have to take, no matter what you have to say. If you have to sack half of the school, sack them, take actions of any magnitude. If you can't sanction them, I will but please for heaven's sake get us out of this murk. Alright?"

"National television?" Bindu inquired.

"Yes indeed. National television," he replied. Muskaan coughed.

And just about then, a visibly shaken up Veenu Sharma barged into Kalsi's office without caring a hoot about who was present inside and who wasn't. She flung a newspaper across Kalsi's table, nearly knocking the glass of water over.

"Did you see this? We are on the front page," she said with an expression that conveyed awe and fear.

Chairman rolled his eyes, "Thank you Veenu for informing us. We knew nothing about it." He said with sarcasm.

"Really? How come you didn't know anything about it?" Veenu asked innocently.

"Please take a seat, Veenu. We have a lot to talk about," the Chairman instructed.

Just a few metres away, the Receptionist of DHS was being heckled by a barrage of phone calls that had been coming incessantly since the news broke out that morning. Majority of India's dailies and news channels wanted to cover the news and gather comments and information. Sick and tired of unending phone calls, she did what she had seen her bosses do all the time – she kept the phone off the hook and in a way unplugged herself, off all accountability on this planet.

TWENTY-NINE

Rishav winced as the studio lights shone onto his face. "Oh God! Switch'em off!" Vanya shouted as the lights hurt her eyes.

"You can't, it's a part of the show," Rishav whispered. "And don't shout for God's sake. It's a studio. And you'll get used to it. Just wait for a few seconds."

"Yeah, yeah. I know," Vanya dismissed him as she covered her eyes with her hands.

Rishav and Vanya were the first to reach the sprawling Headquarters of DNN-IGN located at Sector 16. The journey to the office, which usually took an hour or so from where Rishav stayed, seemed abnormally longer. The thought of facing all those eminent people and Bindu Kalsi was nauseating. Or, so Rishav felt. He was glad that Vanya was sitting beside him. If there was one person you'd want to be with when in need of support, it was Vanya. She could frame the world's most illogical arguments, yet defend the worst of your stands. Although he wished that she would talk less. Already he was nervous and her incessant questions about how she looked made him more restless.

"Chill yaaa. It's gonna be fine. We're gonna rock this studio. And rip BK's clothes off," She laughed.

"Yeah right," Rishav said sarcastically.

"My hair looks fine?" She asked for the umpteenth time.

"Oh God. Yeah. You look amazing ok? Now let me be," Rishav forcefully whispered.

"Pretty boy, why do you get so annoyed?" Vanya slurred. Rishav chose to not pay attention to her anymore.

When they had reached the office, the guard made their passes for entering into the ten-storied office space. The logo of DNN-IGN shone brightly from whichever corner you viewed the building from. Right behind the building was a vast open space which was more than often used for hosting the parties (if one ever happened) and for the coffee vendor and canteen people to set up their stalls for the evening snacks. The two seventeen year olds walked past the number of satellite vans that were stationed outside the entrance to the building. There was also another building, slightly smaller – adjacent to the one that they were entering. It was the Newspaper division of DNN-IGN, which was where Runjhun worked.

The Big Stand was a hugely popular show which aired at 8 pm every weekday. Hosted by famous journalist, Vikki Chandra, the guests who were invited to speak on various motions comprised of the crème de la crème of the society. That specific day, a special motion for a moderated debate on Siddhant Dalvi's life and death was chosen after a lot of cajoling and coaxing by Runjhun, in front of the Ed-in-Chief, Dilip Desai. Although, the TV people were pretty tightlipped on the names on the guest list, Rishav had a fair idea of whom to expect and who not to. Bindu would be there for sure, he thought. It was a live event that would reach over 250 towns and cities all over India. The article on Dalvi's death had already created enough of a furor in the city. The Live telecast of this debate would feed more flame to the already blazing fire, driving the nail straight into the coffins of the DHS management.

Rishav and Vanya were part of the 'interactive audience'. The organisers of the show had decided to put them in the audience instead of having them as a part of the panel since they were only students. But they knew what an integral part both of them would play in this controversial debate hence they put them in the front row of the audience. The assistant producer of the show was there to greet Rishav and Vanya with a big smile. Fakeness, Rishav thought. He warmly escorted both of them around and showed them their production and editing units. Rishav and Vanya sat there in silence in the dimly lit, empty studio of The Big Stand. Some spot boys kept moving things from here to there, apart from that there was no activity whatsoever. Rishav could see the five podiums that were arranged on the stage, the centre one was obviously for the host, Vikki Chandra. The other four were yet to have name plates on them and apart from the obvious choice of expecting to see Kalsi there; he raked his brain to think who else could be invited that day. There was a good hour left for the telecast to begin and Rishav had started to feel a little uncomfortable sitting there with now-so-silent Vanya, all alone. He forced himself to not think of Sahana. To be near Vanya and not have Sahana around was making him restless. Both of them were always together. And now that she wasn't there, Rishav was finding it difficult to talk to Vanya. He thought about whether Sahana would be watching the show or not. Vanya had told him that Sahana knew about the live telecast and she had told her to watch it. He wondered if she would care to listen about what he had to say. *Hell, I am going to make her listen to me and the rest of the bastards*, Rishav resolved. *For you Siddhant, this is for you.*

"We will be on air in ...three, two, one...!" the producer said it out loud in the background.

There was a red signal that flashed 'Applause' as everyone other than Rishav started clapping while the host Vikki Chandra, impeccably dressed made his way through the audience and positioned himself right at the centre of the stage and smiled.

"Good evening all my viewers, welcome to another edition of DNN-IGN Big Stand," the line followed another round of applause as it was directed on the large screen right in front of the audience.

Chandra in his composed self, started speaking as the cameras rolled –not even a hint of nervousness in his voice. "It has truly been a sad week for the people of this city, if not the country. 17 year old Siddhant Dalvi decided to end his life as a result of the alleged harsh treatment that he had been meted out at school. The big question here today is and that is exactly what we'll be discussing for the next hour or so – Who killed Siddhant Dalvi?" He paused to let the question sink in to the minds of the audience. "It's popular belief that schools are becoming institutes of commerce rather than education and the casual, unaccountable nature of its' managements. Is there any truth to it? We'll find out in this hour."

This time around, no 'Applause' sign flashed. "To begin with today's show; I'd like to introduce four very involved and eminent names in this controversy. We have the Honorable Education Minister of India, Mr. Chris D'Souza."

There was a loud round of applause as a short heighted, white haired man in his seventies, walked up to the stage with measured steps. He folded his hands in Namaste as he received the applause.

He walked up to the podium and stood behind it. The camera focused on the next guest.

"Now, we have the lady who is at the centre of this entire controversy, her actions have been much dissected and spoken about. But one must commend her bravery to decide to come on National television and clear the air, ladies and gentlemen, please let's warmly welcome Mrs. Bindu Kalsi, Principal, Delhi High School," Chandra concluded as there was another round of applause. Although it died down far quickly than it had for D'Souza. Rishav scowled as the people applauded seeing the sign on a huge black screen above that said "Applaud".

Fat-ass, Rishav thought, as Bindu positioned herself behind the podium.

Nothing ever seemed to have an effect on her self confidence.

"Welcome ma'am," Chandra said as Kalsi smirked and took her place behind her podium.

"*Kutti*," Vanya whispered in Rishav's ear.

Rishav smiled at her. Chandra took a deep breath, "Okay then, we have two other people who'd have a lot to say about the education system in India and especially about the running of Delhi High School in general. Please welcome the award winning ex-Principal of DHS, Mrs. Meena Singhal and ex-Vice Principal of DHS, Dr. Madhuri Singh." There was a thunderous reception for both of them as Rishav and Vanya exchanged confident glances. They weren't expecting this, but surely the arrival of two of Kalsi's arch nemesis could never be bad. Rishav smiled slyly as he knew how mindfucked Kalsi would get at the end of the show.

Good luck with that, he thought

The countdown had begun...

THIRTY

"Dalvi's death was tragic and it can rightly be called an accident, considering how drunk he was," Kalsi's words echoed on national television.

"Okay, tragic and accident, agreed but where is the whole accountability of the school here? What about a certain Physics teacher who assaulted Siddhant?" Chandra raised a question. "Who? Which Physics teacher are you talking about? I think at this point of time it's better not to allege things at random persons. If they are certain people who are involved in this case their names should be taken clearly," she said in slow motion.

"There had been reports of an incident in the Commerce section relating to Mr. Suraj Singh assaulting Siddhant," said Chandra.

"Suraj Singh is an honourable person and I refute all these allegations, they are baseless..."

"That's not true," Rishav shouted as his echoed in the studio, loudly enough. Chandra glanced at the boy sitting in front.

Trying not to show his irritation in his voice, he looked at him and said, “Audience, be informed that you shall get your chance to speak later.”

“I think it is important at this point of time for him to speak since it is directly related to what has been just said by the eminent Principal of DHS,” Vanya said with contempt in her voice.

“Thank you, Vanya,” Rishav said, getting up from his seat and walking towards the brightly lit stage.

The earpiece in Chandra’s ear, gave him all sorts of instructions, which he wasn’t really following. Some spot boys tried to politely refuse Rishav entry onto the stage.

“Please let him come,” Chandra said, as he heard his producer tell him to invite the boy on stage and let him speak. It would just heat up things and increase their TRPs.

Kalsi’s throat had gone dry. Had she known that he would become such a pain in the ass, she would’ve rusticated him long time ago.

“Get the boy up here, let us hear what he has to say,” Mr. D’Souza said politely.

The cameras were still rolling when Vikki Chandra directed the assistants to plug up Rishav as fast as they could. “We’ll get into a quick commercial break now,” he said. “And when we are back, we shall have Rishav Sen talk about Siddhant Dalvi.”

“We’ll go off air in one two three..!” said the producer as they went off air.

D’Souza, Singhal and Madhuri went into a small discussion as Kalsi used the opportunity to wipe the smeared *kajal* off her face. Vikki Chandra smartly walked up to Rishav who was getting the microphone installed. “Kid, you might not want to do that.

It kills the program,” he said.

"I am really sorry, Sir. I had no intention of disrupting your program but she was outright lying about my friend's death. He was my best friend," Rishav asked.

"I'm really sorry for your loss but we are also here for your friend." Chandra said with his hand on Rishav's back.

"Yes, sir. It won't happen again. So do I get to speak what I want?"

"The moment we are back on air."

"Thank you, sir. I am a huge fan. Sir, can I ask for a favor?" Chandra laughed, "Yeah, sure."

"My friend Vanya saw Siddhant being ragged. I think it would be really good for the show if you have a witness," Rishav said. Chandra nodded, "Of course. I'll talk to the producer." He said and walked towards the assistant producer.

'Back in 120 seconds' – the large screen read. The producer and his assistants started calling everyone back to their places.

"All the best," Chandra gave a parting comment to both Vanya and Rishav after they had been plugged in.

"Thanks," They said in unison.

They were back on air.

"Right before the break, we had little drama as Siddhant's best friend, Rishav made his way to the stage. He has some really scathing remarks. But before we tread that part, let me ask you Mrs. Singhal, are you really satisfied with what you see of the school right now? The very school you took to greatness?" Singhal looked at the camera with a straight face, "Honestly speaking, no. I am highly disappointed of what I see today. Like over-emphasis on music events and shaking off all responsibility and accountability is not something I'd promote. It sets precedence and it acts as a deterrent for growth of schools in the society."

"Point well noted. Dr. Singh, assuming the allegations against Suraj Singh are true, how would you dissect the man and his actions?"

"Let me point this out Vikki, that I regret and condemn Suraj's actions. Working with him closely has exposed to me the rogue nature of his character. C'mon, having connections with X, Y, Z political parties shouldn't be criteria for holding on to your jobs..."

Kalsi butted in, "With all due respect Dr. Singh, you have no right to make such comments that have no proof."

"Bindu, I have every right to point these out. I have been part of that institution and I feel ashamed of the fact that I was. And Suraj Singh's political affiliations are not secrets of the Incas."

"Can I say something?" Rishav asked.

"Yes, Rishav, we'll come to you in just a second. Mrs. Kalsi, you have a chance to respond to that before we move to Mrs. Singhal and then Rishav."

"See, Vikki. I don't want to get into denying these baseless allegations. If at all there were issues with Suraj, someone would have pointed it by now."

"No they won't," shouted Rishav. "That's the whole point, don't you see? They are scared. They don't want to get involved in something as murky as this."

Kalsi shook her head vehemently, "No No."

Singhal butt in, "I completely concur with what Rishav has to say. During my stay as the Principal, I had judged the amount of fear students had for Suraj Singh."

Kalsi rebutted, "Meena dear, Suraj was appointed under your regime. If you so doubted his character, why did you do it in the first place?"

"We are digressing from the issue slightly," said Chandra. "The point here is whether Suraj Singh was to blame or not. No-one is going into the deeper understandings of his character and if at all Suraj Singh was to be blamed, where is the proof?"

"We have proof right here, sir," Rishav said with a sarcastic smile on his face. "Vanya, would you like to say something?"

"Yes of course, Rishav," Vanya said sweetly. "I am in the Commerce section of 11th grade and on November 29th, Mr. Suraj Singh came as the substitution teacher. He assaulted Siddhanth Dalvi right in front of my eyes and twenty others. I think there is no more of proof required to prove that indeed Mr. Suraj Singh, the physics HOD, had committed a heinous offence of ragging and humiliating a student."

If one were to say that Kalsi was humiliated, it would've been the understatement of the century.

"Is the silence worth a thousand words, Mrs. Kalsi?" asked Chandra.

"Moving on, Mrs. Singhal, being an educationist, can you delve into the mind of this teenager?"

"As Rishav said, Siddhant Dalvi was an introvert. He kept to himself and he had a lot of acceptance issues. Why not rake the issue of alcoholism in today's youth? Had he not been pressured by his peer's to take up drinking that fateful day, Dalvi might have lived. Where is the role of the schools here? Why is alcohol available in the hostel?"

"Mrs. Kalsi, you'd want to respond to that?"

"Those photographs had been doctored," she said bluntly, shaking nonetheless.

"Doctored you say, okay then what about the statements of senior clerks in the hostel? I am talking of a certain peon fondly called *bhau*. He admitted to DNN-IGN reporters that indeed he accepted consignments of alcohol," Chandra had mastered his art pretty well.

A flustered Kalsi thought of what to say, "I have no comments on that."

"No comments? Are you sure Mrs. Kalsi? The reputation of your school is at stake here?"

"It is an internal matter and I shall look into it."

"I am sorry to say, Sir but "looking into the matter" is a euphemism for 'we won't do anything'," added Rishav disdainfully. "Strict action needs to be taken and that too now. In a few days everyone would forget what happened to an innocent boy. Next week you would be discussing about another disaster in this very show. The time is now. And I think that principal ma'am should resolve to solve this issue by setting up an enquiry into this matter."

"We will take strict action, Rishav." Bindu Kalsi said as she glared at Rishav. "And as for Siddhant, we will not forget him and ensure that justice is served. There is no bigger loss than having lost a son. And I offer my condolences to Siddhant's family."

"You shouldn't even say that," came Madhuri's response. "You had the audacity to host Socialact Wave and splurge lakhs of rupees."

"We had certain commitments to our sponsors..."

"Sponsors? You didn't even have a clue about what went on. You tried to hush up the matter," Madhuri shot back.

"We absolutely did not. We had to honor our commitments. And we did our best."

"Your best wasn't enough, sadly. I think it would be in the best interest of the school if instead of focusing on organising shows and fetes, the school management focuses on the students and their holistic development." added Singhal.

"I think you have finished your term in DHS Mrs. Singhal and you have no right whatsoever to interfere now," Bindu Kalsi retorted.

Singhal wanted to respond but Chandra intervened, "Digressing again. We have limited time really but what is the solution madam Kalsi? There is a growing rage in the public over your running of the school.

They seek answers, its their children, their money, their faith that you are playing with."

The soft spoken D'Souza who was clearly outnumbered by the ladies, raised his hand to speak.

"Yes, Mr.D'Souza, you want to say anything?" Vikki asked. "Vikki, I want to use this unofficial platform to request madam Kalsi and Shri Chandrashekhar *saab* to give this matter a serious thought and really delve deep into this problem."

"Mrs. Kalsi, a direct request from the education minister himself, before we wrap up, I'd be requiring your response to this." Vikki Chandra directed his statement at Bindu Kalsi who had by now drunk three glasses of water.

Kalsi went into deep thought; she was caught between the devil and deep seas. She had evaded enough of tricky questions that day and had denied continuously. Snubbing the Minister's requests could have dire consequences and in a way affect the ministry's patronage of DHS. She summed up all her courage and weighed her words before she spoke on the mike, "I shall look into the matter personally and put up an enquiry into these unfortunate events. And I assure the family of Siddhant that he will get justice.

In about fifteen minutes, Rishav got out of the studio with a sense of accomplishment. Just about then, his mobile beeped the arrival of a new message. It was a text from Sahana, *You were good* – it read. Rishav smiled and put the mobile back into his pocket.

THIRTY-ONE

"Glad that things worked out between us," Rishav said.

"You really think it has?" Sahana replied, still engrossed in packing her bag.

The noise of students moving out of the classroom and the clatter of desks hitting chairs gradually started receding in the background.

"It hasn't? Haven't I redeemed myself already?" he asked, deliberately slowing down the pace at which he packed his own bag.

"Umm…you have, kind of but uh, I'm not too sure, you know? Like, I really doubt how long this part of you will exist. Who knows this might just be one of the faces of a success crazy Rishav, after all?"

"Ah huh," he chose not to reply more explicitly.

"No kidding yaa," Sahana zipped up her bag and looked up.

Rishav was horribly close to her. It was as though he was

breathing down her neck. She hated it when people stood so close; it just freaked her out – apart from the strained eyes of course. A little indecisive about what to say, Sahana spoke again, "So yeah, you done with packing your bags? It seems like it's been taking you an eternity to get it done." She paused. "I can't wait really long you know? My mom's coming to pick me up today."

"You don't need to wait for long, just a few seconds would be enough," whispered Rishav.

"What?" she seemed surprised.

"I should've said this long time back Sahana, but I never got the right moment. And one thing led to the other."

"Hmmm…" she said.

"Are you listening to me?"

"Yeah yeah, carry on," she replied.

"Sahana, you are one girl who's touched me a way no-one else has," he said while she indicated him to start moving towards the door.

They walked slowly towards the class door, with a lot of uncomfortable silence between them.

"Sahana," said Rishav, as they stood right next to the door.

She raised an eyebrow.

"Sahana…" he took a deep breath. "…I love you," he added.

Her expression didn't change till a tiny smile appeared, "I know." She said. "And I've known it for a long time."

EPILOGUE

Bindu Kalsi quite reluctantly agreed to set up an enquiry despite her tall claims on television. Although the findings of this enquiry were never made public, certain tough decisions were indeed taken in the light of the recent happenings.

Suraj Singh was put on notice under immediate effect and his political connections became a subject of a lot of scrutiny. Muskaan Kaur was transferred to DHS Porbandar as its Principal, with the Chairman heralding the move as 'strategic brilliance'.

Bindu Kalsi resigned from the post of the Principal of Delhi High School, owning moral responsibility for all that had happened under her leadership. She even took back the school's official stand about Siddhant's suspension, before she stepped down.

The Chairman made a remark about how power is best in the hands of those who don't want it and subsequently transferred the responsibilities of running Delhi High School to Ms. Veenu Sharma.

Veer Chauhan was politely asked to step down as the school's trustee and the hostel warden was sacked. His Highness Jai Chauhan no longer considers the school to be his paternal property. He is still the sole Head Boy of Delhi High School.

And as far as Rishav and Sahana were concerned, it was hard to say whether their story had ended or whether it had just begun...